D0975028

# THE USE OF FAME

(A NOVEL)
## CORNELIA NIXON

COUNTERPOINT
BERKELEY

Library of Congress Cataloging-in-Publication Data
Names: Nixon, Cornelia, author.
Title: The use of fame : a novel / Cornelia Nixon.
Description: Berkeley, CA : Counterpoint, [2017]
Identifiers: LCCN 2017005018 | ISBN 9781619029491 (hardback)
Subjects: LCSH: Married people—Fiction. | Domestic fiction. | BISAC: FICTION
   / Literary. | FICTION / Family Life. | FICTION / Contemporary Women.
Classification: LCC PS3564.I94 U84 2017 | DDC 813/.54—dc23
LC record available at https://lccn.loc.gov/2017005018

Jacket design by Jarrod Taylor
Book design by Neuwirth & Associates

ISBN 978-1-61902-949-1

COUNTERPOINT
2560 Ninth Street, Suite 318
Berkeley, CA 94710
www.counterpointpress.com

Printed in the United States of America
Distributed by Publishers Group West

10 9 8 7 6 5 4 3 2 1

# THE USE OF FAME

# ONE

"WHAT'S THE USE of all this fame if we're not getting laid?" asked Johnny, leaning his chair back on its hind legs.

Ray was eating, so he just looked at him. The night before, they had read together at the 92nd Street Y, and now they were at a deli in the Garment District, a place that made good grub, okay for a guy like Ray, who grew up on top of a coal mine and knew what he liked. He was scarfing a Reuben, salty grease of pastrami in his mouth, cut by the acidic crunch of sauerkraut and the sweet, creamy Russian dressing oozing down his chin. Between bites, he had just needled Johnny about the girl he saw him put into a cab that morning, outside of their hotel—she looked about twenty-three, Japanese and tiny, with long, silky black hair. There was a party for them after the reading, but Ray had left early, went back to the hotel, called Abby, and turned in. Johnny must have met her after that.

Ray chewed fast and swallowed, so he could talk. "So, who was she anyway?"

Johnny didn't answer, only shrugged.

Ray shook his head—it was like Johnny still wanted to be the guy he was decades ago, when he had hair, and Ray's wasn't shot with white. When Ray could run twelve miles in the hot sun, have sex three times a day, and his face was never gray, the way it had looked in the mirror this morning.

Johnny pointed to the dressing on his chin.

"Yeah, yeah," Ray said.

Jesus, Johnny was as finicky as Abby, who would have handed him a napkin. Johnny didn't come from coal mines—his dad was some kind of lawyer, and he ate like a girl. He had barely finished a salad.

When he polished off the Reuben, Ray whisked the bread crumbs from his fingers and wiped his chin with the back of his hand. "So. Why do you do it anyway? Aren't you afraid of wrecking it with Sarah?"

Sarah was the woman Johnny had been with for years, a nice outdoorsy nurse, and he had finally married her the summer before. Of course, Johnny was weird about his space and kept a separate apartment, so he wouldn't feel crowded. In Gainesville, where he taught, he and Sarah had places a few blocks apart. Ray couldn't imagine it. When he and Abby taught in the same city, they slept together every night, breathing in sync, parts of them touching, sometimes dreaming the same thing. They had been married almost twenty-five years, and he slept the best like that.

Johnny set his chair down lightly and peered at him. "What? Don't tell me you're getting old. It's a choice, you know. Women are big medicine. You should give it a try. What about that Tory girl? You know you want to."

Ray sat up straighter and ran both hands back through his hair, to make it stand straight up. Yes, he had told Johnny about one of his grad students, a lovely girl who was imprinted on his brain. But he wasn't going to talk about that now.

"You know I don't do that," he said, with a dragging in his chest, like chains pulled through.

Johnny laughed. "You sure as hell used to. Remember when you couldn't go to the Porthole anymore?"

It was true, before Abby, yes. Ray had spent nine years in Morgantown, as an undergrad, then working, then grad school, and the place had many lively bars, which he got into at first with a fake ID. Often he picked up a girl, slept with her once, and never called, which could make it tricky to go into certain bars. In those days he had straight blond hair down to his waist, and chicks seemed to go for it. It helped, too, that he lifted weights, which gave him shoulders on an otherwise linear frame. ("Mr. Stark has a flat butt," his first-grade students tittered later on, when he was a Poet in the Schools.) He was still skinny, but losing the shoulders—compared to the past, he could barely lift these days. His heart was giving out, with probably the same condition that had killed his dad in his forties.

"Did you walk in here?" a new doctor had lately asked, the first time she saw his test results. But at age fifty-two, he could still swim half a mile and work out on contraptions in the gym, way beyond heart-patient level—no one could explain it. As far as he was concerned, that meant doctors were just guessing about his heart.

But being sick was not his style, and he would fight it all the way. Just not how Johnny would.

Johnny watched him with a grin, still living in the past. "I always thought girls went for you because they wanted your looks. Jesus, that hair you had? It made them think theirs might get better if they only slept with you. Plus, you had the moves. You told me your

3

technique. Of course you were witty and charming, and after a while you'd lean back casually. If she followed you, she was hooked, and you could kiss her right away."

"And now that's what you do?"

"Learn from the masters. But really, you could still get away with it. You know the women in that audience last night were there to get a look at you and swoon. I bet half of them can barely read."

Ray sat up straighter, looked away—this was just Johnny's way of needling him back. Johnny knew he hated it when anyone mentioned his supposed looks in connection with the work. He wanted to be a disembodied wraith, who left words like fairy shit on the page.

It disturbed him, how readers wanted poets to look good, maybe because they all stood on stages, reading into microphones, giving talks at conferences. Still, this wasn't Hollywood, but were there any ugly poets being read these days? Ginsberg in the fifties, yes, but no one he could think of now. Well, at least he was getting older and funnier-looking every day—he'd started to get nose hair he had to trim, and though he kept his mop short now, the coarse white threads made it extremely unruly. "What was his hair doing?" his students asked each other, about some sighting of him. If people bought his books anyway, that meant they really liked the work.

Johnny was still talking, not having noticed Ray said nothing back. "You know you haven't changed. You're still an ecstatic type. You just express it differently. Remember Fucking Houdini?"

Ray suppressed the urge to smile—that was a night, all right. He had been what, twenty? Still getting into bars as Eugene Cassini. He and Johnny were in college then at West Virginia U, and that night they'd been doing shots and snorting coke. When the bar closed, they went out into an alley, where Ray took a piss against a wall. He was still splashing pee when a cop car turned in, and two guys got out and cuffed his hands behind his back, just as he felt the need to puke. He didn't want it in his hair, so he crouched, lowered his bound wrists, stepped backward over them, raised them up his front over his head and down to the back of his neck, where he caught his mane into a pony tail and held it back.

"Jesus, we've arrested fucking Houdini," one cop said, and took him away to book.

It was not the only time Ray ended up in jail. He had contempt for moderation then—he wanted to fly, and in fact did, jumping out of planes too many times to count. He'd get stoned on dope or coke, ride some rattletrap into the sky and be the first one out, screaming as he fell, and wait till the last second before he pulled the cord. There was nothing like it, and he never wanted it to stop. For a while, to finance it, he had sold dope to frat boys, till the night his supplier laid a gun on the table. That was his first whiff of mortality, but he'd had plenty since. These days, if he woke up in the night, he looked straight into death.

Johnny squinted at him, like he was too far away to see. "You used to quote Baudelaire to me, as you ordered the eighteenth round for everyone. 'One should always be drunk, with wine, with poetry, with virtue, as you choose. But get drunk.'"

Johnny kept going on about that for a while—he could be a bit of a village explainer, and in his new hearing aid, way loud—his workshop students must have felt a bit browbeaten. Johnny was sure of himself for good reason—he was smart as a whip—but students didn't respond that well to whipcracks.

And women—how was he still getting them? Well, he did look pretty good. Johnny was a big, broad-shouldered Viking with impish eyes and a rueful smile, below a wide, full, platinum mustache that completely hid his upper lip. It was such a good mustache it seemed to make up for the fact that his formerly reddish hair had disappeared, leaving a gleaming head of skin, and young poetry wannabes tried to copy it. Some chicks were maybe willing to overlook a bit of explaining to get close to Johnny and his famous 'stache.

When he finally paused, Ray said, "Notice he doesn't mention girls."

Johnny shook his head as if in disbelief. "He doesn't have to. It's implied, whatever gets you high. For me it's finding out about strange women, what they're like, the endless possibilities."

Ray shuddered, imagining the complications, how scrambled he would feel. He needed an empty mind to write, every morning of his life, to let language grab hold of him and fling him into outer space. That was the ecstasy he needed now: the riot of words, their insanity, and what you could make them do or do to you. Johnny had reviewed his last book, and it was a great tribute—he had called him "a fire engine of language," though Ray thought he'd rather be its arsonist. He wasn't into rules, conventions, traditions—he liked to disrupt them. That meant people didn't always get his poetry, but that was by design—he wasn't writing for the bozos. Death-Ray Stark, that's who he was, a suicide bomber in the marketplace of poetry.

Funny that he and Johnny still liked each other. Johnny wrote more conventional stuff, often focused on the news, about some question like the overuse of therapy or climate change or consumerism in America. His style was plain and clear, no tricks—he thought everything in a poem had to have a reason, or possibly even be reasonable. Didn't Wallace Stevens already make a debacle of the rational, not to mention Rimbaud?

But Johnny made no sudden moves of the kind Ray liked, no experiments with words. Johnny tried hard to tell the truth, about whatever he observed, and his own unreliable feelings. He was cynical as hell, but at least he could be funny, too, in a sly, ironic way. The night before was the first time they had read together, and it went off pretty well. They had picked on each other and got some laughs. He felt Johnny scrutinizing him.

"You know what?" Johnny said. "You were lucky. You found a woman as good-looking as you, who could be your twin sister, in fact, and she was not some dumb blonde. And you got to marry her. You got to marry the love of your life. Most people don't."

Ray's sick heart lurched—he reached for his glass of beer. Was Abby still that? It was true, when she had first showed up in Morgantown, as young Professor McCormick, tall and willowy in a pencil skirt, he had fallen hard for her. He had never wanted anyone so much as he did Abby then (or not till now—but he put that thought aside). Abby had liked the important stuff: beer, grub, sex, and him. She laughed at all his jokes and loved his work. He couldn't get enough of her.

She was eight years older than he was, but she had never looked it, and even at sixty, she was still pretty, and so deep inside of him he might never get her out. She was his life, in fact. She had anchored him for decades, and losing her would be like death, of who he was.

So what the fuck was he doing now? For a year, he'd had it bad for Tory Grenier, and it felt like eating his own liver. Yesterday she took the train down from Montreal, where she had moved after leaving Brown. They had walked around the Upper East Side, holding hands, and kissed for the first time, on the street. But then he sent her back. He could never stand up to read into a microphone if she were there.

Johnny shook his head. "I don't get you sometimes. You're a conundrum. A guy who flings himself out of airplanes, and sleeps with a hundred girls, then just one woman for half your life? I can't imagine it. It would threaten the structure of my personality. I need more room to breathe."

"And you don't think you're a conundrum, too? Or an enigma, better still. It's true of everyone, even to ourselves."

Johnny shook his head. "You're no enigma, pal, and neither am I."

That cheered Ray up—he loved to argue with Johnny. "Oh, yeah? Tell me one true thing about myself."

"Sure. You're a touchingly needy person. That's why you've hung on to Abby so hard, and why you don't, shall we say, develop other interests. You're afraid you'd fly to pieces if you lost her."

That arrow hit Ray's solar plexus, but he didn't let it show. "That's because you think personalities have structures. I'm already in pieces, and so are you. I can't be contained in any envelope. I explode in all directions. And you? You're nothing but contradictions. You need space, and when you get some, a whole hotel room to yourself, you find some girl to fill it up."

Johnny knitted his brows. "You're taking that too literally. And you're sure as hell contained in the envelope of your marriage. That's the thing I couldn't stand, and that's always been true of me. And you're the same person from one year to the next. I've known you, what, thirty-three years? And you've always been Ray Stark, a recognizable entity, not just physically. Something's holding that together."

"I don't think so," Ray said. "There's no structure in me. I might be needy one second, but also not needy at all, and the next I'm solitary as a turtle. I'm more like a tornado, a typhoon, colliding atoms and chaos. And the reason I don't sleep around is so I can try to find the eye of the storm."

THEY LEFT THE deli and walked briskly south, in the cold November air. Ray was glad they could still walk at least, long-legged with big strides, both of them in jeans and beat-up running shoes. Ray had on a threadbare overcoat, while Johnny wore a cardigan, bald pate lidded with a black beret.

They made it to the Strand, where it smelled of old paper and ink. They showed each other books they liked or hated, and talked about the friends who had shown up at the reading and the ones who couldn't, because they were too far away, teaching at Texas, Arizona, or Iowa—people Ray knew from writers conferences, and readings, and because other poets had introduced them to him. Some of them were as bad as Johnny when it came to women. They operated like the sloth brain of the poetry world.

Hank, for instance, who was Ray's colleague at Brown—Hank had slept with a lot of girl students. He used to work the oil fields in Montana, and he still drove a beat-up pickup truck, but now he wrote fine poems about the ocean and its mysteries, about dolphins' songs and gliding, glinting schools of fish. They had helped him win Priscilla Duffield, a beautiful and elegant woman whose work got the kind of attention Ray didn't even want. Who needed rave reviews in the lying *New York Times*? And poems in the *New Yorker*, with its bland suburban taste? Though Priscilla's weren't bland—they were dense and allusive, philosophical to the point of being almost impenetrable—Ray was sure they flummoxed matrons everywhere.

Maybe the editors at the *New Yorker* just had the hots for her (and there it was again, the confusing of talent with looks). They had printed a full-page photo of her face, and Ray and Abby saw it once in a furniture store, cut from the magazine, framed, and propped on a side table.

Priscilla was only five years older than Ray, but she had a lot more clout in the poetry world—she used to be in charge of the program at Brown. Hank had come a long way from the oil fields, and he and Priscilla led a glamorous life, with good-looking kids, a big house on a brick street in Providence, and a place on Martha's Vineyard, where to be invited was almost as big an honor as the Guggenheim. But did that stop Hank screwing around? Ray knew because Hank talked about it. At Brown everyone seemed to know, and probably Priscilla did, too.

This had gone on for years, until Priscilla had enough. She started her own affair, not with a student but with a Stanford poet named James Poore, and she conducted it right under Hank's nose. Poore stayed with them on the Vineyard, bodysurfed with Hank, masqueraded as a family friend, and wangled a job offer for Priscilla at Stanford. The semester she decided to go, Ray and Abby had sat through brunches, dinners, late-night drinks with Hank and Priscilla as they argued, she maintaining she was doing it only to send their kids to Stanford free. The argument was still in progress after her first year in Palo Alto, and Hank got so worried he stopped chasing girls. And then, six months ago, Priscilla had flown to Jamaica, snatched a quick divorce, and married Poore.

Priscilla happened to be in New York the night before, and she came to the reading—but she knew better than to bring Poore, since Ray was close to Hank, who was still crushed. After the reading, she came up to the podium and kissed Ray's cheek, looking like a blond Audrey Hepburn, in a red dress and flats, her very short platinum hair freshly shorn and bleached. He had studied her face in fear—she had been married to Hank as long as he and Abby were. Was she happy now, or did she no longer recognize her life?

He didn't know Priscilla well enough to ask her that. But that's what he was afraid of—that he would maim the marriage, be sorry, and never get it back.

He pulled her new book from the Strand poetry stacks and showed Johnny her picture on the back. "Do you think she's happy now?" he asked casually.

Johnny made a *pfff* sound with his lips. "How would I know? I'm not one of her anointed."

Ray shoved the book back in its slot. "Neither am I."

"Oh, right. She gave you a big prize and a job for no reason."

Ray's jaw tightened. This fall, he was teaching in place of Hank, who was on sabbatical, but that was unusual. "It's only spring semesters. Fifty-two years old, and I don't have a real job."

It was time for the bigger honors to start showing up, or at least for fuck's sake full-time work. He wanted to teach all year, with power and prestige. Back home in Mules Ford, West Virginia, his mother bragged that he was an Ivy League professor, and he had to correct her all the time.

Johnny picked up a book by a guy they knew. "And what would you and Abby do if they offered you full time?"

Ray felt a slow burn in his chest. Abby taught at Berkeley now, a dizzying six-hour plane ride away from Rhode Island, and most years he spent eight months out there with her. Seven years before, he had tried to stop her taking that job, the same way Hank tried to stop Priscilla, and now the results were falling into place. Would he have gotten so hung up on Tory, if Abby had stayed where he was?

He had always been proud of his beautiful wife. Abby had the kind of looks that meant guys had been hitting on her hard since she was twelve, and they all wanted to marry her. She had even said yes to two of them, briefly—it was back in the 1970s, when everyone else was taking lover after lover, but Abby had married them instead. Her first husband was a society bloke her mother had dug up, the second some doofus she met in grad school. Ray felt sorry for them, she'd unloaded them so fast. And since he married her, he'd had to fend off other guys, other poets, especially the older generation, famous men who could be sexist clowns.

"Va va voom," one of them had said to Ray, the first time he met her.

One night at a party in New York, Ray had introduced her to a covey of four men, all literary heavyweights, and right in front of her and him, they had discussed her looks, as if she were an art object.

"A young Grace Kelly," one of them had declared.

"I see Katherine Hepburn," another said.

Ray'd had to muscle in and put a stop to it.

And where was she now? Three thousand miles away—anxiety raced through him at the thought. These days he wasn't always exactly sure what she was doing, when. After she moved to Berkeley, she had started riding horses, out of nowhere. She claimed she did it as a kid and always wanted to again, but he'd seen no sign of it for their first twenty years. Now she was out of the house for hours at a time, taking care of horses, riding them, not giving a damn about their life. Full time. He couldn't even get his marriage to go full time.

"HEY," JOHNNY SAID, now in the poetry stacks, and cuffed him on the shoulder, as if to wake him from a trance. "Any news from Miami?"

Ray felt the urge to do a full-body shudder, like a dog shaking itself. That fall, he had been invited to apply for an endowed chair in Miami, and they flew him there for an interview. He was waiting for the short-list call now, hoping to use it to put the screws to Brown and get them to give him a full-time job—it was what he had been told to do, by his mentor, Walt. Walt was an older poet more famous than all Ray's other friends combined, and he taught at Harvard and knew how things worked in academe. He said the way to get promoted was to apply elsewhere, whether you wanted to leave your present post or not, because if you got an offer, you could use it as leverage. It was like those experiments with monkeys, where they don't want their own banana, they want someone else's. He was going to become someone else's banana and make Brown want him more.

"What happens if Brown doesn't fall for it, and you end up in Miami?" Johnny asked. "You'll be closer to me."

Ray felt the worry knot up his forehead. "I don't know. It would be more moola, and a bigger statue of me in the town square, for dogs to pee on. But it's weird, there's part of me that wants to stay at Brown, in a program run by marmots, because—can you see me inflating my frog neck?—it's the fucking Ivy League."

Johnny cocked his head. "Yeah, I get that. But if you come join us peons down in the swamps, what will you and Abby do?"

Ray shrugged. He knew one thing for sure, it was Abby's fault. Abby's fault he had ever looked at Tory Grenier. And whatever happened next, let it be on her.

Suddenly he noticed a new book by that shit Whitney Ames, the incompetent jerk who had replaced Priscilla at Brown. He yanked it off the shelf and felt himself boil over like a pot of milk forgotten on the stove.

"This asshole!" He shook the book at Johnny. "You know what he did? He had the goddamn nerve to flunk my best student, a brilliant girl. Tory, he flunked Tory Grenier and made her cry! I read that paper, too, and it was fucking great. She dropped out of the program because of it. One of these days, I'm going to go cut off his head!"

And there was Ames's picture on the back of the paperback, self-satisfied and smirking. Farrar, Straus and Giroux published this shit!

Gripping the book in both fists, Ray tried to rip it in half. It was a slim volume of verse, but surprisingly well made. He tore off the back cover, then the front, took hold of the back pages and jerked hard—they came away. He yanked more handfuls, threw them over his shoulder, until the book was thin enough to tear in half.

Johnny laughed. "Um, you going to purchase that?"

"No way." Ray ripped up what was left, threw the pieces in the air, and stalked out of the store.

# TWO

ABBY STOOD IN the Denver airport, gazing out at the fading light. On the runways, snow lay heaped, and more was coming down like rice tossed at a bride. The agent at the desk had just told her nothing was flying east, a blizzard all the way to Providence. They could get her there via Dallas and DC, arriving the next evening.

But tomorrow was Thanksgiving Day. Johnny and Sarah were flying up from Florida, and Hank was coming, too, Ray no doubt already up to his elbows in rice and rosemary and chorizo, for his signature stuffing. The turkey would be brining in a mixture of kosher salt, sliced oranges and lemons, whole sweet spices, garlic, herbs, and gallons of water, double-bagged in a big cooler, weighed down with pounds of ice. He would have Brussels sprouts still on the stalk, ready to snap off. This was his favorite holiday, since it was solely based on food, and they had always cooked for friends.

Abby was supposed to show up, too, of course, but she had taught that morning in Berkeley, and this was the fastest she could get here, what with taking a run to unwind after class. Okay, sure, she could have run at dawn, but before class she had to tweak her notes, trying to be less of a fraud. Who had time to read every word written about James Joyce and still remember all the details in that doorstop of a book? She'd wake up from dreaming that she had to give a lecture, naked, on something she hadn't read, in a room she couldn't find; get out of bed; make coffee and revise her notes; then scramble off to Wheeler Hall and try not to have a panic attack as she walked into class.

Right now her big slouchy purse was crammed with other people's new research, and the only thing worse than reading it would be to do it at 4:00 A.M. in the Dallas airport. All to show up at Ray's for the end of dinner, by which time the three male poets would be bellowing at each other like walrus beach masters, having put away about five bottles of red wine. Then they would grab each other's necks, knock foreheads together, and declare, "You know I love you, man. You know I love you."

Now in Denver it was completely dark outside, and she could see her reflection in the glass—she critically examined it. The body was still mostly slender even in a heavy sweater, though she had stopped counting calories somewhere along the line and put on twenty pounds. And the face was like a history of everything that had befallen her: a deep furrow between the brows and a crease down the left cheek that could be mistaken for a scar, left by a six-year illness that had gone as mysteriously as it had arrived. (Doctors had called it lupus, but lupus could kill you, and Abby refused to believe that's what it was.) Her hair was expensively maintained light blond to hide the gray, but its former rotini curls were now mere waves. It had started to relax after her mother died, and straightened more when her closest friend was killed—as if too much grief were chemotherapy, affecting your fast-growing cells, along with your brain. Her brain was definitely not the same.

She turned away so as not to have to watch herself, and called Ray on her cell. She told him about the blizzard and the poor flight options.

"No, don't do that," he said. "That sounds awful. I'll be home next week anyway."

Surprise left Abby slightly breathless—she had expected irritation at least. "Are you sure? I could get there for the end."

"No. It isn't worth it." Now he did sound mad. "It's because you're so fucking far away. I told you it would be like this!"

She let a beat go by without reply, not wanting to start a fight. He always blamed her for the distance between their jobs—when in fact, after she got the job at Berkeley, he was offered full-time teaching at San Francisco State but had turned it down—he said because it was too much teaching and not enough money, though probably it was also not enough prestige. At any rate, they had both chosen to live this way.

His voice softened. "But that's too long to spend on planes. Can you get a flight back to SF?"

"There's a seat on one about to go."

"Then you should grab it."

There was something odd about his reaction, but she was so relieved she rushed to the agent at the desk. Fifteen minutes later, she was buckled in the last remaining seat.

It was a little dicey taking off from Denver in the falling snow, feeling the wheels slip, and bumpy on the climb over the Rockies to the west—Abby was not a placid flyer, and first chance she got, she ordered a stiff drink.

Waiting for the drink, she suddenly missed Ray intensely. Out of her purse she took a talisman she liked to carry, a snapshot that was slightly blurry, like the past itself. It was of her and Ray from a quarter century before, two tall, skinny, young blond people who appeared impossibly happy, radiant and beaming, outdoors under a big tree. She had her back to Ray, his arms around her from behind, both of them suntanned and laughing, in matching white T-shirts printed with red strawberries, won when they ran the Strawberry Canyon race in Berkeley on their honeymoon—she with her T-shirt tucked into her jeans, which she couldn't even remember ever doing. She had always been short-waisted and long-legged, and she had to diet hard to dress like that—these days she wore long shirts that deemphasized that area. The race had run from the Cal gym up a wooded fire road steep as a waterfall, to the top of the Berkeley ridge, and on the way Ray had contracted poison oak on his private parts by taking an alfresco whiz, which interfered with the honeymoon but made them laugh. The photo was almost frightening to look at, as if so much beauty and happiness were dangerous to see. They might have been a pair of tall white cranes or ibises.

Still, she loved the way the picture brought back Ray in youth. The first time she saw him, her first semester at WVU, she was still reeling from the difference between Berkeley and Morgantown, where guys hung Confederate flags in the windows of their rusted nothing-to-lose-mobiles. She felt closer to the grad students than the faculty, who kept inviting her to terrible dinner parties, where there would be three of her new colleagues, all older men, with their wives and some poor single guy they had fished out of Morgantown to introduce to her. Most of the candidates they found were gay, and she and whoever he was would gaze at each other balefully from their separate corners of the table. She instantly forgot all of their names.

After one such deadly dinner, she had gone to a grad student dance party, still in a proper skirt and blouse and heels, while jean-clad grad students parted around her like the Red Sea. Her students were all there, some playing poker in a side room, while the young male MFA poets goofed around, inventing a dance they called the Wandering Foot. About midnight, Ray blew in, tall, thin, and cool as David Bowie, with the same cocky, self-ironic way of walking, like he knew he had it but was also laughing at himself. Twelve-pack under one arm, he strode across the room so fast his old tweed jacket billowed behind him, all the other poets giving him high fives. Immediately, Abby thought, *That guy's trouble.* So of course she couldn't take her eyes off him.

A few months later, she was lonely on a wintry morning, driving to the natural foods co-op, when she saw him standing on a street corner in falling snow, gazing down at a girl in a fuzzy pink angora cap so tenderly that it made Abby ache. Why didn't she have some-one to look at her like that?

The final straw was the night she went on a blind date with a young philosopher who had lately published a border-crossing book about artificial intelligence and art, which was academically respect-able and yet on the *New York Times* bestseller list. The philosopher had told one of Abby's colleagues he was looking for "a tall blonde with brains and something sparkly about her," and the colleague had arranged it. Abby hadn't read his book—how could she, when she was teaching a graduate seminar on literary modernism, the reading list all monstrous tomes? She was supposed to know not only those books, but all the criticism on them. She was starting to realize she would never actually be prepared for class and would have to wing it. She wondered if her Cal teachers had winged it, too, but she doubted it.

But she was lonely and agreed to meet the guy at a so-so restaurant, knowing at least he would be smart. Over dinner, the talk was heavy sledding—he didn't drink or loosen up in the course of the meal, and nothing was fun or natural.

Afterward he suggested they go hear jazz at a bar, and Abby wanted a drink, so she went. They sat at a small round table on a raised level of the floor, slightly frozen over beers, listening to a local quartet. They had been there half an hour, Abby hoping to find a way to go home soon, when five MFA students came tumbling in, laughing and exuding playful energy: two couples and Ray. One couple was a bit dressed up, the girl with a bouquet of pink roses, and Ray looked extremely good in an ironed white oxford shirt, black jeans, and high-top sneakers, with a pink rosebud between his teeth. The others sat, but he stood beside the table, half turned toward Abby—light seemed to shoot from his blue eyes. He kept the rose in his teeth and gazed at her with gentle comprehension, as she sat so mournfully with her stiff date.

Within months they were lovers, thank God. Ray had made her laugh so often then, like the time he wrote her a letter while playing Copeland's "Fanfare for the Common Man" and said it was hard to type with both hands in the air, conducting all that brass. When they were apart, he wrote her every day, and he liked to hide little notes around the house. At first he had called her String Bean because she was five ten, and that had evolved to Bean. On their first Valentine's Day, she opened her underwear drawer and found a drawing of a green bean and a lit match, signifying his incendiary self, and in the match's thought balloon was a big red heart.

People didn't understand about commuter marriage, that it could be romantic, writing letters, then glimpsing the beloved waiting for your plane. Most years they were apart just one semester, and that was not so bad, since one of them flew across the country every few weeks. It helped to keep it fresh, something you could miss. Maybe in part because of it, Ray often made great declarations, even after all this time.

"If we were ground to powder, our molecules would find each other," he had said not long ago. Once from Providence he wrote to her, "My love for you did its sneaker wave on me again this morning. I felt a flush of joy and traced it to its source and there you were. Lucky me."

They never fought about the things that troubled other couples. Ray liked to cook and clean, and had ever since their second night together, when she briefly left him in her rented house and came home to find vacuum-cleaner lines in the carpet. He had a sense of humor in disasters, like the time a chicken he was roasting caught on fire—he grabbed it and ran it out into the snow. He was also a great nurse, who'd helped her through the mystery illness for six years. Nurturing seemed to give him a sense of purpose, as did housecleaning, a use for his dervish energy.

"You're not allowed to clean anymore," he had long ago declared, after he watched her dust. "You go in with a flaming sword. It's not worth that much."

It was true, she was a perfectionist, and it was hard for her to do anything halfway, no matter how trivial. Once she had asked him, "How did we ever make it this far, when you're an ecstatic, and I'm OCD? Not exactly a match."

Chuckling, he had replied, "It's only physical."

Or was perfectionism just another form of immoderation, like ecstasy? On a deeper level, it was possible they had recognized themselves in each other, both of them excessive, wanting too much, expecting too much, giving too much or not at all. Irresistible forces crashing into immovable objects.

And these days, if the sex wasn't what it used to be—well, Ray was in his fifties and a heart patient. But it was still good, and they probably had more of it than couples in their third decade who lived together all the time.

AT SFO, SHE retrieved her car, drove home to Berkeley, and called Ray. He'd been out for pizza with Johnny and Sarah, and he sounded like he'd had plenty to drink. He told her what he still needed to do for the dinner tomorrow.

She felt overwhelmed with guilt. "God, I'm so sorry I'm not going to be there."

"Never mind," he said, briskly. "You tried. How do you make that great cranberry sauce of yours anyway?"

"Don't cook the cranberries. Just put them in the Cuisinart and whir them up raw with a quartered orange. Leave the peel on. Then add a little sugar, maybe a quarter cup, and some chopped walnuts."

Suddenly he flipped into rage. "Jesus, I'm going to kill Whitney Ames. I can't believe he had the nerve to flunk my best student! She dropped out of the program because of it. That asshole will be lucky if I don't cut off his head!"

Abby was puzzled—every late-night phone call lately had gotten around to this. She tried to use a soothing tone. "Sweetie, you've said it all before. Why don't you write him a letter or something?"

"Oh, that creep, forget it. I read that paper, and it was great."

"What's going on, sweetheart? You say that every night now, and you sound so angry and arrogant."

Right away he said, "I've always been angry and arrogant. You used to like it."

Well, at least he wasn't mad at her, and eventually she talked him down enough that he could go to bed.

When they got off the phone, she made herself a nightcap and sat on the couch, worrying. Why was Ray so irascible lately? There was his heart, of course—he said he was in pain all the time. And they were having to be apart too much this year, both semesters instead of only one. Maybe that could explain the late-night rants.

But other odd things had been happening. A few weeks ago, he had asked her to go to New York with him, for the reading with Johnny, and of course she wanted to be there. She loved his poetry—it was the thing that had really hooked her on him. When she heard him read, she fell for him all over again.

"It's quite an experience sitting next to her while you're reading," Walt had told Ray, one time when he and Abby were both there. "She vibrates like a lightning rod."

So she had bought a ticket for New York. But a week before the reading, Ray had called and said, "Don't come. There are people I need to see. I won't have time for you."

So she canceled the reservation just in time to get her money back.

And then, two days before he was to go, his voice was panicked on the phone. "You have to come to New York with me! You have to!"

"But I canceled the reservation. It'd cost a fortune to get there now."

"I don't care!" he cried, like he was hyperventilating. "You have to be there!"

So she had priced a new ticket—thirteen hundred bucks. Certainly not worth it, since she'd have to fly right back to teach.

So she didn't go. And what was worse, she had planned to get to Providence tonight, just a week later, for Thanksgiving tomorrow, and now she wasn't going to be there, either. She felt another rush of guilt, and knew why—she was secretly relieved. There was knowing what Thanksgiving dinner would be like, Ray no doubt defaming Whitney Ames and forcing Hank to promise him a full-time job, though Hank was not in charge the way Priscilla used to be. And Abby would have at most three days before the long flight back.

And best of all—most guiltily—not going meant she could take care of her horse. The grooms had holidays off, and if owners did not show up, horses spent all day trapped in their stalls, with their blankets on, even if it got too warm. But now she could take Beau out and let him run around.

Before she went to bed, she sent Ray a text so he would wake up to it. "I'm so, so sorry not to be there, sweetheart. I miss you so much."

Funny that Ray texted now—he had always been a Luddite technophobe who used a manual typewriter for his poems, banging them out with two fingers. He didn't own a laptop or even use a copier. He retyped his work every time he sent it out, always changing it. Sometimes when a magazine accepted a poem, he didn't know which version they had until he saw it in print.

Then suddenly that fall he had started texting all the time, and he taught Abby how. She liked the way it made no demands but let you get to it on your own time, like email only more immediate, on the phone—he said his students had taught him how. He also started using her laptop when he was at home, sometimes late at night. Well, it was 2007, and Brown, like Berkeley, expected profs to be on email every day of the year.

* * *

THAT NIGHT SHE slept well, glad to be in her own bed and not in some airport, drinking bad coffee as she plowed through other people's research. In the morning she made outstanding coffee in the French press and dispatched two articles, before putting on her breeches and driving a half hour east of Berkeley, to the barn.

The stables lay in a narrow valley, hills on three sides rising up so high that black cows grazing near the tops resembled poppy seeds. Gold in the summer, the pastures were now green from the first rains, with dark oaks in the ravines and sheer rock on the steepest slopes, under blue sky and white clouds.

The barn had stalls for ninety horses, and most stood with their heads over the gates, watching for humans. Beau was close to the parking lot, and his big shining brown eyes followed her, ears pricked, as she left the car. When she approached, he called with a deep throaty rumble, ducked his head and pressed it to her chest, nuzzling her hands with his velvet lips as she kissed his broad forehead, taking in his clean horsey scent.

"God, that horse loves you," Ray said the first time he saw that, and it always made her heart feel hot.

Quickly she removed Beau's blanket. He was a beautiful dark bay, brown with black mane and tail, long slender legs, a white star on his forehead, and one white sock.

The horse in the next stall was freaking out. Still with his blanket on, he reared on his hind legs and looked longingly over the top of his stall like he wanted to jump out. Abby took his blanket off and led him outside to a paddock, where he immediately bucked and reared and ran around. She led Beau to the next pen to keep him company, then went in search of other horses equally stir-crazy and took them out, too.

Soon a general festival of bucking and rolling was in progress out there, horses with happy ears, forward and alert.

And it was not just fun for them—it was important, more so than most people knew. Horses could die of colic, caused by eating standing still, trapped in their stalls. They were supposed to walk as they grazed, and if they didn't, their guts could twist.

It had happened to Abby's first horse, one terrible night. She and Ray were eating dinner when she got the call, and he refused to go with her.

"You don't give a damn about our life!" he had yelled as she rushed out.

But he had no idea how fragile horses were, how fast they could succumb. After midnight, she called him sobbing from the large-animal ER at UC Davis, where they said the horse would not recover, and lethal injection was the humane thing to do.

On the phone, Ray had started to cry. "I am so sorry I'm not there with you, I could kill myself."


**TODAY SHE LEFT** the others outside while she clipped Beau into a set of crossties in the stable, to pick his hooves and curry and brush him, as her mother had taught her when she was five. She had always loved the peace of barns, the sound of swishing tails, sighing nostrils, flat teeth crunching hay, and the green smell of fresh manure and piney woodchips in the stalls. High up in the rafters, sparrows flitted through, chirping as she tacked Beau up and led him outside to a mounting block, where she swung into the saddle and walked him out into the sun.

In the biggest outdoor arena, size of a football field, she warmed him up through walk, trot, canter, then let him open up and gallop for a while, before she took him for a cool-down walk on a hilly trail. He was angelic the whole time, clearly feeling privileged to exercise, when most of his herd could not.

It was almost dark by the time she got them all in, groomed and blanketed and in their stalls. But she drove home content and called Providence.

"Heeeeeeey, honey," Ray said, expansive and happy, men laughing around him. Music throbbed on his sound system, some kind of independent rock.

"Jeez, do you have a wife, guy?" Johnny yelled over the singer's voice.

Johnny's wife, Sarah, wrestled the phone away. "Where are you, lady?"

"Didn't he tell you? I was snowbound in Denver, and the only way out was west."

Sarah made an exasperated sound. "How could you leave me here alone with all these lunatics?"

Behind her, walruses were barking.

"They'll never give me a full-time job!" Ray wailed.

"Yes, they fucking will!" Hank shouted back. "Even if I have to kill someone!"

"You? You've never killed anything," Ray said scornfully.

"Ah, man, you're wrong. I wish you weren't," Hank said, sounding drunk.

"What did you kill?" Ray cried, in a way Abby had seen many times—no one upset, because it was their sweat lodge, where they'd tell each other things they had held back before. "What did you fucking kill?"

Hank's voice cracked. "I had to kill my dog."

"What? You had to kill a dog?"

Johnny cut in. "Of course he did. Don't you read anything he writes?"

"Sarah?" Abby said.

Sarah grunted, obviously listening to the guys as well. She was a no-nonsense person, who wore hiking boots under her long white wedding dress, when she and Johnny married on a cliff top in Maui. It was a small event, and Abby and Ray had rented a white convertible to be the getaway car, blasting a tape of Pavarotti as they swooped along high cliffs to a hotel lunch with the families, before the four of them went snorkeling at Honolua Bay, chasing sea turtles. Best wedding ever, they had all agreed.

She could hear Ray in the background. "How does a guy who grew up eight thousand feet high in the mountains end up writing about fish?"

"Man," Hank exclaimed. "That high up, it is the ocean. It was the ocean floor. And you know it's that extreme we're going for. The edge. The farthest out."

"The fucking limit!" Ray said ecstatically.

Then it got quiet, probably because he and Hank had grabbed each other's necks and were silently butting foreheads.

Johnny got on the phone. "You can't leave him alone like this. We count on you to keep him calm. You're the goat in the stall with the racehorse."

Abby knew racehorses had animal buddies, often a goat. *Why a goat?* she wondered, though they did seem wise, if you looked into their small green eyes.

# THREE

RAY LOVED HIS funny little house in Providence. It was about a hundred years old and had belonged to a fisherman—so simple, there were no halls, just rooms that opened into each other, a staircase straight into his bedroom, a tub in the kitchen. But all that meant little privacy, and Johnny's need for space made it too much for him. So he and Sarah had booked a room at a B & B, and they were leaving in the morning to cross-country ski in Maine.

So Ray had the day after Thanksgiving to himself. He slept late, snoring with his mouth open, shaking off the wine, then got up and contemplated the kitchen, which they had all just abandoned at God knew what hour the night before, turkey grease and cranberry sauce across the counters, empty wine bottles. He was pleased with how the meal had gone, turkey moist and succulent, good as it got, his dressing damn good, too. If he trusted his instincts, his cooking worked, because he obeyed no rules, took the top off the rice and stirred it while it cooked, never measured anything, and fuck the prissies who predicted otherwise.

He put on the CD of John Zorn, *Naked City*, cranked the volume up, and buzzed around, cleaning up the kitchen. A few leaves of Brussels sprouts had gotten ground into the maple floor he and Abby had installed, and that she had quickly ruined, in her impatient way, carrying a dripping broiler pan across it, leaving a line of black grease imbedded in the wood.

They should have had the new floor shellacked, the way they did in their first house, in Morgantown. When they bought that place, it had ugly cigar-brown shag carpeting in every room, but Abby had pulled up one corner and thought she spied hardwood beneath. When they went to Berkeley for the summer, she had someone come in, rip out the carpet, refinish the floors, and shellac them. When they got back to Morgantown that fall, the house was filled with gleaming light oak floors.

That place was beautiful, small but peaceful, on a dead-end street with a huge yard. He had planted thirty-six flowering trees and bushes and five hundred bulbs, pink frilly daffodils and black irises and Emperor tulips that came up magnificently every spring, and red, white, and pink peonies that flourished their ruffles in June. He missed it and their life in Morgantown, walking through the alleys of his youth.

Why had it not been good enough for Abby? When he finished grad school, he had landed teaching in Pittsburgh, just seventy miles away, and they had a decent life, together almost all the time, though he kept a room in Pittsburgh to cut down on the drives.

But no. Abby had to go back to the Bay Area, to her family in Pacific Heights—as if Ray wasn't her family now—and Berkeley, where she did her PhD. She needed to impress her former profs and spew theory jargon. And when her mom died and left her a pile of money, she bought a pricey condo in Berkeley's Gourmet Ghetto, where you could get twenty kinds of mushrooms, strawberry papayas, and organic frisée even in December, when only iceberg and apples might be had in Morgantown. She threw around another bundle on a Porsche, color of a buttercup and far too pretentious for West Virginia, so she could style around with the top down. And after a while, there were the horses, too.

And if Ray ever objected, she would put her perfect retroussé nose in the air and say, "It's my money. I can do what I want with it."

And yes, Ray loved Berkeley, too, the way the fog crept in all summer long, chilling the nights even if it was scorching at noon. August, when it stayed gray and cold, like morning all day, no pressure to do anything but write in his café. Views of the bridges, San Francisco white and hilly across the bay, sailboats drifting by. Yeah, yeah. Everyone was so cool out there, Ray felt instantly more suave the moment he arrived. Sometimes he even loved the Porsche.

But that wasn't who he was. Not one goddamn other person out there grew up over a coal mine. Berkeley people all had perfect teeth, but his family could not afford dentists, till they had to have their teeth yanked out and wear dentures. No one in Berkeley ate even the best venison, let alone the roadkill kind (though it was lean, high protein, free of additives, and economical), or fried catfish, or all-the-way dogs.

But all right, when Abby got her dream job and took off, he landed one almost as good at Brown, a big step up from Pittsburgh, even at half time. And there were working-guy bars in Providence, places where he felt at home. Real people, too, some of them his grad students, guys who'd scrambled up from some godforsaken place like him. And yeah, Tory, a petite brunette with a tiny waist, from

Montreal. Her father was a butcher, who had stopped school at four-teen and never really learned English.

Quickly he checked his phone.

"Beignets for breakfast. Yum," Tory had texted him. "Did you survive the night, darling?"

"Barely," he thumbed quickly back. "Tackling kitchen now. Wish you were here. I'd take off all your clothes so fast."

"Send," he pressed, and stared at the kitchen counter, imagining how he would start, if she ever came in through his door. After New York, he had sent her a silk blouse, pale pink to set off her coloring, and he pictured her in it, how it would feel under his palms as he stroked her small round breasts.

He thought of how he had walked around the city, holding her slender hand. The top of her head came up to only about his heart, her smooth dark hair trimmed neatly at the bottom of her jaw. He had sat across a little table from her, trying to memorize her face. The big intense brown eyes, the beautiful nose, not like any he had seen before. A little long, a little arched, but soft and tender-looking, like a baby's. Her mouth was wide, lower lip more full. The way she lifted her light hand and let it fall open in an explanatory gesture was the most graceful human act he'd ever seen. He had missed what she was saying, watching that.

To steady himself, he pulled Abby's worn-out copy of *The Joy of Cooking* off the top of the fridge and flipped to a recipe for beignets. He would never make them—he made guy stuff, though not just kick-ass pizza and burgers—he did risotto and paella, too. He loved cook-books, the only tales with happy endings guaranteed. But he never consulted them, except to catch an idea, blow it up, and make it new.

You could say that was, right there, the difference between him and

Abby: she read recipes and measured everything. She also used perfect grammar, tried to make him learn it, too, and she could spell—she broke his balls over that all the time. He was dyslexic, okay? And his relationship to language was alive and real—he wanted to dive into the flaming magma at its heart and let it spit him out. Who cared how the fuck you spelled the words? Someone had just made that up, a couple hundred years ago. It was not a moral issue. It was arbitrary, dead.

Just to spite her, he got out the milk carton, put it to his lips, and poured it in his mouth. Abby was voluntarily three thousand miles away, and that meant he did stuff his way. He spent all the money he wanted on CDs, though she sometimes ragged him about that. He said, "The lawn needs mowed." He said, "I'm going to go lay down." He said, "Give it the fuck to Hank and I." He spelled the sink implement *spong*. He'd had to train Abby: if he yelled from his study to hers, "How do you spell *perception*?" she was not allowed to lecture him on Latin roots or handy rules to help next time. She was just supposed to shout, "*P-E-R*," et cetera, though Ray thought *preception* made just as much sense.

In their early days, she had been stuck up from her la-di-da grad school, and he had to call her "Berkeley" and beat her down in arguments. It helped that he had published fifty poems by the time they met, while she had nothing but a contract for an academic book. Sure, his were in tiny magazines with names like *Blue Porch* and *Fish,* some of which folded soon afterward. But they still got into print.

He also had to correct her attitude about her colleagues in the English Department at West Virginia U. She thought they were all idealistic people, who could have made a lot more money as doctors or lawyers but chose to teach because they believed in it—when actually they were Ivy League shits who hated Ray for being working class. One of them had ripped up his paper on experimental poetry and tossed it like confetti at his head, shouting, "Quit! Just quit! You can't do this!"

But soon after Ray finished his MFA, his first book was bought by a major press, something the confetti guy could only dream about. He also married Abby, Confetti's prized new colleague, and snubbed the man every chance he got—until, at a party for young faculty, Confetti had apologized and asked Ray to dance. Ray accepted the apology, though he declined to dance.

**NOW, IN PROVIDENCE,** he changed the CD and blasted Van Morrison as he washed every dish by hand. He didn't own a dishwasher—didn't want one in the house. Abby probably used the one out west when he was gone, but he didn't believe in it—those things wasted water and did a lousy job. And if there was a spot of food left on a plate after washing it, he rubbed it off with a dish towel. Towels went in the washer, didn't they? But when Abby saw him do that, it drove her mad.

"You don't believe in the germ theory," she had said to him accusingly.

He had laughed at that. "It's not a theory, it's a fact."

He had started out as a premed, and he loved the human body, its heart like a big knot, a plucky pump that shoved blood cells through hair-thin capillaries and back to itself too fast to watch. He loved the microscopic creatures that lived all over him, and the frass that bugs left on the molding he had painted white with loving care when they first bought this house. Poor Abs, parts of the place gave her the creeps, it was so far from Pacific Heights. In the basement a toilet seat sat on a hole in a cement block, leading to a sewer pipe. It still worked, but she never went near it. She used the prissy little powder room recently stuck on the back of the house, and she disinfected everything. She refused to eat his mother's cooking after she watched her taste gravy then stir the pot with the same spoon.

"I'm just not afraid of bugs, is all," he told her. "You shouldn't be, either. They're all over us in billions. They are the stuff of life. Relax."

When he finished the kitchen, he used lemon spray on a rag and dusted everywhere, stopping once to check his phone—nothing more from Marie-Victoire Grenier. He loved it that she spoke two languages—he himself was a second-language speaker in English, his first being Grunt and Squawk. But Tory could rattle off in French the same as English, and it sounded slangy, joking, imitating voices—he'd heard her on the phone with her dad. That was the way to speak two languages, not like Abby (who had studied four, all of them correct), but the way that people talked. Language was alive. People changed it all the time, and to nail it down was to kill it, like it would a snail.

Abby had understood that once, or had a prayer of doing so. Before she went to grad school, she wrote poems. It was all she wanted to do, and when she showed up in Morgantown, she revered Ray's work and him because of it. She'd gone to get the PhD only because some shithead professor told her she was better at research than poetry, and she believed him. But her poems were damn good. She didn't want to show them to Ray, but when she finally did, he was impressed.

"You've just never put the energy into it the way you do with literary criticism," he told her then. "You can't do it on the side. You have to give it all you've got."

Abby had looked scared when he said that, but she started doing it. Right away, her stuff was accepted by good magazines and made *The Best American Poetry* twice, before Ray was picked once. She still had to sweat out getting tenure, but she was a very disciplined worker, and she got the Joyce book done on time. On her tenure sabbatical, she wrote only poetry, and magazines took most of it.

Then suddenly she had won a contest, had a book of poems published, got good reviews. Johnny read it, called her up and said, "You are so good, you should not be let out on the street. You should be chained to your desk."

So then people started asking Ray and Abby to read together, and to teach at the same writers conferences. They were turning into some sort of goddamn literary power couple, and the future had looked great. If they'd stayed in Morgantown, it might have been.

But then one of her old Cal professors had finagled a job description perfectly fitted to her and told her to apply. He put together a coalition of English profs and got her the job—without tenure but with two years to the decision.

Abby couldn't pass it up, though it meant virtually the end of poetry for her. To get tenure at Berkeley, she needed another book, and Cal was so heavy into literary theory it could not be poetry.

So instead, as soon as she took the job, she read truckloads of French crap and spouted lines like, "The name is to the psyche as the erect penis is to the body." And far worse shit, sometimes in such heavy jargon he couldn't translate it. By the time she got tenure again, she had a fifth language, literary theory, and friends who spoke little else. *Positionality*, they said. *Discourse, semiology, phenomenology, subjectivity, patriarchy,* and, oh yes, *gynesis*. God, how he hated stuff like that.

HE THREW THE tablecloth, napkins, and kitchen towels into the washer and ran it, removing all trace of Thanksgiving. He paced the house, furiously running hands through his short, bristly hair. He stared out all the windows with a sense of menace, something coming toward him. But all he could see was gray sky, patchy snow, gray trees.

Next week, when he went to Berkeley for the break, it would be only December, but the pink magnolias would start to bloom, and camellias. Some roses never stopped. Dungeness crabs would vigorously fight each other in the fish markets, and in the backyard of their building, the Meyer lemon tree would be loaded down with thin-skinned fruit that was almost orange, almost sweet.

God, he wanted to be there. That much would be clear, the pure pleasure of the place, in early spring. And the wonderful used book and record stores where he could browse for hours every day—they were an education in themselves. Thanks to Moe's, he had devoured unknown books of poetry, and big volumes on art, atomic physics, the French Revolution, outer space. Berkeley made him feel like a hummingbird, zooming around, ready to grab a new idea, or make love, burst into song.

Why didn't he go west for Thanksgiving? He could be at his desk right now, with its slot of San Francisco view, typing up what he had scrawled by hand that morning in his favorite Berkeley café. In a few hours Abby would quit working, go for a run, take a long hot bath, and Ray would pour them wine and sit beside the tub on a tall stool, mulling it all over with her. They would cook together, drink more wine, maybe watch a movie, or he would, while she read by his side.

The thought filled him with warmth and peace, then dread. What was he doing here, three thousand miles away? What prize made it worthwhile to wager Berkeley and Abby and their life together? It was who he was.

*Bing*, went his phone, where he'd left it, on the kitchen counter, and he jumped away from it, the snake in this garden. He turned it facedown, so he wouldn't have to see what it said: *New message from*

*Tory Grenier.* Did the people who invented texting know what it would do for infidelity? He had sat next to Abby, texting Tory. Abby slept later than he did, and he and Tory wrote back and forth before she stirred. Was it a game, to spite Abby, like drinking milk from the carton? Or did he really want to ruin everything?

He was a loon, married for life. Where he came from, if you found The One, you stuck with her. The search was over. She became your family, more even than a blood relative, because those you didn't choose. You picked your wife, and that made it indelible.

Abby's views were lighter, flightier—she came from San Francisco, where it was a wonder anyone stayed together long. There had been those two early divorces, and whenever it got rough with him, she was always ready to pack her bags. She claimed her move to California had not been that, that it was just the job, just loving Berkeley, and being closer to her family. But this was the result. This was the result!

He pulled out the heavy vacuum cleaner, fired it up, and shoved it around to work the anger off. By the time he stopped, his head was clear, and he felt an old familiar ache and glumness, missing Abby. In a week he could put his nose in her hair. Would it be enough to make him forget the girl?

He checked his phone again, but there was still only the last message from Tory ("I miss you, too, darling"). Of course it wasn't Thanksgiving in Montreal, and she had a bookstore job all day. But they talked now every night, and he had been dreading what it would be like with Abby there and having to sneak out on some excuse to use the phone.

WHEN THE HOUSE was clean, he made decaf, since he was no longer allowed caffeine, put on a new CD, and sat down at his ancient kicked-in desk, trying to write, but it all just came out crap. Waiting for the inner peep, which had been drowned by the speaking peep, the night before. Feeling stupid and dull, late November in his head.

So instead he read the pile of stuff for his grad workshop. There were some surprisingly fine poems in it, a few of his students strange beginning creatures with lanterns in their skulls. They needed only to get both feet a half inch off the ground at once for them to make a miracle.

But this semester, every one of them was a chicken in the workshop except Zack. They were all afraid of him because (a) they thought he'd read everything, because he made wild generalizations and said something about Chaucer or the Pre-Socratics; (b) they'd probably read nothing; (c) Zack was arrogant and without tact (but when he said something was "sloppy writing" in Jonah's poem he was right!); and (d) they thought of themselves as tiny flowers.

Ray's job was to convince them they were dragons. They were saddened by the thought that not only were they insignificant, but it was hard to write poetry, and writing poetry was insignificant. But, hey, then what did they have to lose? What was there to be afraid of?

He wasn't going to scribble on their work just yet—something Johnny said last night was rankling him. He had made a crack about Ray's latest book, that it was full of poems he'd done before, all the same moves, and why didn't he try writing in a different mode? Ray blew it off at the time, it was so absurd, but now it made him mad. Johnny thought he was predictable, good grief! Had he looked at his own work lately? No surprises there. The nerve of the big galoot!

He put on a crazy Corigliano symphony that featured duck calls and police whistles and God knew what else, rolled a clean sheet into his beat-up typewriter, and banged out a letter with two fingers, holding nothing back. Johnny's work was all bloody identical, the mixed emotions, self-doubt and deprecation, irony and insight and awareness of evil. But the sameness didn't matter—it was brilliant, and sometimes it made Ray feel like the top of his head was coming off. By the end of the first page of his letter, he was praising Johnny's work, while rejecting the terms of Johnny's criticism of his own, along with his understanding of language and poetry in general. He needed to be set straight about that for sure.

The letter felt cathartic, therapeutic, and when he finished it, he put it in an envelope, addressed it to Johnny and applied a stamp. Changing into sweat pants, a T-shirt, running shoes, and a windbreaker, he took off out the door into icy air that smelled like snow, ran to the nearest mailbox, and shoved it in. Then he loped across the ridge above the town, to where Brown sat, all haughty red brick on its hill, across dry grass and patchy white on campus lawns. The sight of his building made him instantly angry—fucking Whitney Ames, he could strangle the guy with his bare hands. But maybe he'd show him, if he got the job in Florida.

He ran down the hill on the other side, dodging traffic through old streets, and kept going till he could see the docks.

He was almost there when something grabbed his heart, hard like a boney hand, and squeezed. Pain shot through his core—he fell to his knees. He couldn't breathe. Was this the moment his heart quit? All right, so be it. At least now he couldn't wreck his life. He stayed there gasping, on his knees, waiting to black out, as cars whizzed past, stuck-up academic swells in Volvos and frat boys with ski racks on their Jeeps, no one noticing.

From a sooty brick building across the street, a dockside bar, a big-bellied man rolled out, scratching his beard, two others behind him in the dark doorway. "Hey, mate, you all right? You want we should call 911?"

He could barely make out the guy's accent. But thank God for the working class, always there when you needed them. He struggled to his feet and waved.

"Nah. Just hungover," he called, and the guys laughed and raised their mugs.

He made a note of the bar's name, the Jolly Whistle, to come back sometime. Or who knew, the stiffs in there might beat him up, if they found out he was a pantywaist poet, making his living at that great sow on the hill.

He walked home, not pushing it, turned into his untended yard, through the busted gate in the weathered picket fence. Maybe he'd paint it all come spring. Or not.

When he opened the front door, the house felt suddenly too empty, cold, and echoing with loneliness. He dropped onto the couch, picked up his phone.

"Cleaned up the mess," he texted Abby. "Heart not worth a crap today. Feels stupid to be here. Miss you. Wish I was there with you."

She didn't answer—she was probably not looking at her phone. She was probably out on her horse, not even thinking about him.

So instead of waiting for an answer, he sent one to Tory, too. "Cleaned up the mess. Heart not worth a crap today. Feels stupid to be here. Miss you. Wish I was there with you."

# FOUR

A MONTH LATER, on the night before New Year's Eve, Abby flew back from the MLA Convention in Chicago, where she had given a paper on "James Joyce and the Female Sublime." Ray picked her up in the Porsche at SFO, and they drove back to Berkeley, to their favorite French bistro. It was cold and raining out, but cozy in the half dark of the restaurant, with its open kitchen tended by chefs in tall white hats, warming the room with smells of cassoulet and crème brûlée.

They ate crab-stuffed sole in cream sauce and sautéed spinach with currants, and drank a bottle of Frog's Leap sauvignon blanc. Ray seemed in a good mood, but he did not say much—Abby studied him in the candlelight. He'd become very thin lately, and tonight he was all in black, black long-sleeved T-shirt and jeans and a black jacket. He looked slightly manic, blue eyes shining, the emerald in one earlobe twinkling. He'd always wanted a tattoo, and she had talked him out of it. But she had given in on the earring and bought it for him one birthday.

Once she might have asked what he was thinking. But he always claimed not to be, that if they weren't talking, his mind was like a silent cave, where a water drop occasionally fell. *Plink.* Her own mind was never blank. It might only sing some golden oldie, daydream, or argue with a stupid question about her work. But empty, no.

Suddenly his eyes filled with tears—she saw his contact lenses start to float.

Alarmed, she touched his hand. "What is it, sweetie?"

He shook his head—his voice was choked. "Remember the baby jays?"

She gripped his hand and grinned. It was in their early days in Morgantown, when they were those two impossibly young and happy people in the blurry photograph. Their first house was a small rental backed by woods, and one spring they heard what sounded like a dot-matrix printer in the yard, going *eek eek eek.* Then one dawn, sunlight threw the shadow of a nest onto their bedroom wall, four tiny heads weaving with open beaks. Later the babies grew blue fluff and learned to fly, three of them staying off the ground, with one poor fellow down too low, making feeble hops.

"Yes. Hoppy," she said. Until Hoppy found his wings, they had rushed out to shoo off cats that came into the yard.

Ray shook his head, as if trying not to cry. "Remember how they talked to each other?"

"Yes, of course." It wasn't in commanding caws, the way they sounded usually, but in the softest coos.

Ray caught the waiter's eye, ordered an Armagnac for himself and a Lemon Drop for her. His eyes were still suspiciously shiny, and she wondered if he was about to start his evening rant. She almost wished he would.

Quietly she asked, "Are you okay, honey?"

He shrugged. "I feel like shit most of the time."

"I'll make you an appointment with Dr. Death." That was what they called the cardiologist who had given them the awful news, ten years ago.

Ray's face went hard. "He can't do anything. He'll just talk about a heart transplant. I'd rather die."

"Oh, don't say that, please. I need you to live."

The sweet drink arrived, and she put it to her lips, sucking the sugar off the rim. Tears suddenly bulged her own eyes, surface tension only holding them, haloing every candle in the place. "A downhill scenario," the cardio had called Ray's prognosis, if they hadn't caught it in time. Two years, the doctor said he would have had. Two years till cardiac arrest, probably while running up a hill. It was breathtaking to hear—Ray would have been dead now for eight years.

They had found out only because his mother came to visit, and Ray had complained of chest pain—it was always something when he was exposed to her. Once they went to see her back east, and within two hours, Abby had to take him to the ER with violent stomach cramps—they gave him tranquillizers, and the two of them went home the next day. It was years before he told her the truth, that his mother had abused him as a kid. Once, when he was six, she had smacked his face so hard his glasses flew off, hit a wall, and broke, and he had to fix them himself with duct tape so he could see. She did things like that for years, and now his body seized in some way every time he saw her, though he was always fine when he got away from her.

But Abby wasn't going to mess around with chest pain—her father had died young of a heart attack. Ray didn't want to go, but she made him an appointment with their doctor, who ordered a stress test. On the treadmill, Ray's long legs ate it up so fast people came from other rooms to watch. But two months later, he was about to go teach at a writers conference when their doctor called their landline, and Abby answered it.

"I showed the results to two cardiologists," he said. "There's something wrong. He needs an echocardiogram."

"Okay," Abby said. "He's leaving for ten days, but he'll do it when he gets back."

"No," the doctor said. "He has to do it now. Today."

That was their first clue. The echo showed his heart enlarged and half filled up with muscle, too little room for blood, and too weak to eject it normally. With each contraction, a normal heart pumped out about sixty percent of the blood it held, but Ray's ejection fraction was twenty-eight percent. He canceled the conference gig and spent a day in the hospital for thirty thousand dollars' worth of tests, including a heart biopsy through his carotid artery, while Abby sat nearby with Janis Joplin singing in her head. *Take another little piece of my heart now, baby. Take another little piece of my heart.*

Idiopathic hypertrophic cardiomyopathy, the diagnosis was, and for ten years now he'd been on meds to rest his heart and help it heal. It had shrunk enough that he was allowed to run again, though he could do much less than before, and he had to see specialists in Berkeley and Providence. The past few months he'd complained of feeling tired, unable to run well, and she'd noticed he seemed to be dieting, doling out a handful of almonds for breakfast like a fashion model, sometimes drinking a foul brew called Kombuchka instead of beer.

"I'm getting rid of my girl fat," was what he'd said, and he now weighed less than he had in his twenties. These days he wore his hair just long enough to flare around his head, and above his stick-thin frame, the overall effect was like a lit sparkler.

Worried, Abby watched him. "I wish you didn't have to leave so soon. You're going to be away too much this year."

He had already been gone all fall, replacing Hank, and soon he had to leave to do his regular spring semester at Brown.

"You know I want a full-time job," he said.

She decided not to remind him of the job he had turned down at SF State. "That would be wonderful. You know I'd be delighted to teach less. I could go half time. I might even retire and live with you all year."

For decades, she had carried a full load. And of course he wanted a better job, now that he was famous for his work.

"What's Hank saying about the job?"

Ray's face went pale and grim. "He says it's in the bag, but I'm starting to think he's a lying two-faced jerk."

"Oh, honey, don't say that. You know he's on your side."

Ray raised his hand, signaled the waiter for the check, and when it came, she looked away—he always overtipped, glad for the chance to be generous. He liked to buy rounds for his friends and bring home gifts she didn't need, clothes she'd never wear—sheer shirts and cheesy earrings. It was a clash of styles, hers preppy and classic, when Ray hated plaid. Plaid! Maybe because, though the Scottish clans were dirt-poor warriors, in this country their insignia reeked of privilege, like his students at Brown. Well, Abby had gone to Smith, and she loved tartans, Black Watch and Stewart especially, for the juxtaposition of colors, crosshatch of lines, the reassuring repetition of pattern. But she'd had to give them up.

They had plenty of other differences—their taste in movies, for instance. In the old days, Ray went with her to the film society in

Morgantown, then made fun of the black-and-white Czech films she liked. At home, every night, he searched the tube for stuff she couldn't stand, about exploding heads, zombies, or aliens. That was the most astounding thing about him, that he watched such junk. He and Johnny both did, and when they were together, they went to theatres and actually paid money to see things like *Alien 3*. In fact, Ray owned the entire series.

Was it something about their West Virginia roots that made them like such stuff? She could not imagine what its pleasures were. The one horror movie she had seen scared her, and she didn't like to be afraid.

She had worked it out with Ray—he could watch what he wanted, with the sound off, so she didn't have to listen to the screams. But he refused to use earphones for the music he played extremely loud when he was home, and she had learned to tune that out, except for the pieces that she liked. That included everything by Iron and Wine, especially the one about *One of us will die inside these arms*, which she took as an anthem about her and Ray and how they would be together when one of them died.

THEY DROVE UP the hill to their apartment, where it smelled of lemon oil, because Ray had cleaned that morning before he picked her up at the airport. He hung up his jacket in the hall, and Abby walked into the kitchen. On the counter was a postcard from Johnny to Ray, manually typed, all lowercase.

```
i admit that when i got your rather excessive
reaction to my suggestion about writing
something of a different mode, I thought that
```

```
you were a little excoriating, but sarah
said that your letter was in fact diplomatic
as nine horses on amphetamines being pulled
back at the camp town races with concertina
wire, so I decided not to send you the long
blond braid hairpiece of a little heidi girl
throwing a hissy fit in her wading pool.
And then I heard that the catholic family
values council had already censured you for
heretical thinking and I thought, aw, poor
ole guy—no boat, no oar, harem desertion
imminent—send him a poem. Odysseus, your wife
is on line 2.
```

She was laughing when she felt Ray come into the kitchen behind her. "What's Johnny chiding you about?"

When he didn't answer, she turned—he looked wild-eyed, his hair electrified.

He took a step closer, one hand over his heart. "I'm in love with someone else."

"What?" she said, still holding the postcard. Then she heard it. She was almost too astonished to speak.

"Who?" she finally breathed faintly, and felt ridiculous. What did it matter who?

His eyes, still wet, half popped out of his head. "Tory Grenier. I'm a dismal cliché, in love with a grad student." He looked at her and begged. "Do something. Yell. Hit me. Stick a knife in me."

Trying to oblige, she threw herself against him and smacked his chest. "In love? How dare you? You couldn't just fuck her, you had to fall in love?" But that felt fake—she dropped her hands and started to cry. "I only did that because you asked me to."

She went to their bathroom, splashed cold water on her face. How could she have been so stupid, after all those rants? That was symptom number one of love, talking too much about someone. And the sudden texting, the diet—signs so obvious, no women's magazine reader would have missed it, and how did she?

She went back to the kitchen, where he still leaned against the sink, looking almost frail. "Do you have a hankie?"

He pulled out one of the dozen she bought him each few years, fine white linen.

She blew her nose. "Tory is what, twenty-two?"

"No, she's older," he said quickly. "More like thirty. She was out of school for years. She's been married."

"Half my age."

She could almost forget she was eight years older than he was—people assumed they were more or less the same. But now that she had crested sixty, what did he do?

He didn't answer, and she remembered something he had said, on one of those telephonic rants. "I thought she lived with her boyfriend. Steve."

He shook his head slightly. "She's breaking up with him."

"For you. She's breaking up with him for you."

He didn't answer that, either, and Abby stood up straight. "You should go to her. Pack a bag. I'll take you to the airport now."

Ray looked panicked. "No. What are you talking about? I haven't slept with her! I've kissed her exactly once. I'm not a creep. Here, let me show you what I'm not."

He strode to his study, came back with a piece of paper, and handed it to her. "That's Hank's instructions on how to have an affair with a student."

1. Don't send mixed messages.
2. Make sure the girl knows it's just for now and you will not leave your wife.
3. Don't tell your wife.
4. Leave no evidence. Be very careful with emails, credit-card and phone bills.
5. Swear the girl to secrecy. She can't tell even her best friend or her mother. Nobody.
6. If you think there's any chance she won't be able to keep quiet, end the thing.
7. Don't be an asshole. Don't tell your wife.

Abby felt disgust at Hank, and exhaustion and grief. She gave it back to Ray. "Thank you for not being Hank. It was very brave of you to tell me. No wonder you've been so insane. You must have been in pain."

He stared at her and gave a strangled sob. "I thought you would be so mad. How can you be kind to me? You should hate me, that's what I deserve. It would be so much simpler. I can't stand it that you're being kind."

RAY'S STUDY HAD a bed in it, and he slept in there, while Abby gazed into the dark from their big bed as astonishment and disbelief gave way to shame. With sudden clarity, she saw herself: she was a ridiculous person. All her life had been a quest for love, and now she had lost the only guy who'd ever given her enough. He had convinced her love was not a sham, that men do sometimes love you back and even stick around when you're being a jerk. With Ray the love had felt inexhaustible, a steady source of happiness, like a spring that bubbled up inside of her, constantly renewed. Twenty-five years of that. Losing it would be like having something amputated, all that mattered of her life.

It was just too hard to believe. Ray had never had a midlife crisis, and he'd been devoted to her all this time. Beyond romance and sex, he had shown real love for her. Back in Morgantown, the initial diagnosis of her mystery illness was "poisonous spider bite," and Ray had washed every piece of clothing, every curtain, blanket, and throw rug in hot water and bombed the house with exterminating aerosols. He found a gap in her closet that opened to the crawl space, boarded it up and posted a sign with a picture of a spider in a circle, crossed by a red line. When her joints swelled so badly she moaned in her sleep, and her eyelids became red blisters, he had carried her from the bed to a hot bath every morning.

When her rheumatologist declared it lupus, Ray was in the room, and Abby didn't notice he was crying till the doctor handed him a box of tissues and told him he could wash his face next door.

When he left, the doctor said, "He's a good man. Some don't take it so well."

Abby had missed a beat. Ray, a good man? She thought of him as sexy, dangerous, talented, and smart. But good?

She shrank deeper into the bed—did she really want him to stay? The truth was, there were times when she had fantasized the end, and no one would blame her if she left him now. She hated to admit it, even to herself, but there was a flip side to his love and had been almost from the start. Before their wedding, he had been intense, but playful and charming, the way most people saw him all the time.

But afterward, she seemed to slide into the place of his mother, whom he loved and feared, and he had started to control her. It was one thing to know that an abused child would grow up to be that way, and another to have him tell her what to do and demand to know where she was every second of the day. He loved it when she slept late, immobile in bed—it made him feel secure. But if she went out and did not come home the instant he expected, he turned into an abandoned infant.

"Where the fuck have you been?" he had shouted too many times to count. Once when she came home late from caring for her aged mother, he heaved a bottle of Liquid Paper at a wall, splattering an aureole of white on blue—they had to repaint the room. He had never hit her, but in one of their worst fights, he had grabbed her purse and dumped its contents out, and in another he had thrown her keys out a window.

And yet, in the mornings, he could be the sweetest man. His smile was like a child's, pure innocence, when he brought her tea in bed. No matter how bad the fight, he could reverse emotions, enraged one second, wry the next. He made fun of himself. "Here I am on my puny pulpit, setting the world straight!" he might cry after a rant.

Gradually, she had given up the things that threatened him. He refused to share her with anyone, so they had no kids. If he didn't like a woman who might become her friend, saying she was crazy, or untrustworthy, or too aggressive, Abby gave her up. He asked her to remove all trace of other men, though it meant tearing up the pictures of her first two weddings and honeymoons, the first in Italy, the second barefoot on a local beach, when they were grad students and broke. She used to think of herself as a free-range animal, for whom the globe wasn't big enough to roam—she loved to travel, ski and surf, climb mountains, but Ray wanted only to stay home. Finally she had started riding horses, because it was an adventure she could have nearby, with other women, and still get back in time for dinner, to keep him calm.

But even if they stayed home, he could melt down, in part because of how he drank—well, both of them drank, it was something they shared, leftover from their carefree younger days. One year, back in Morgantown, when she had the mystery illness, she had quit and discovered the true boredom of their social life, the evenings in front of someone's woodstove, while the others turned their blood to wine. Two couples they knew had weddings that summer, and at both events she was the only guest still trying to converse while everyone else did the Watusi in a conga line around the pool. So of course as soon as she was well again, she rejoined the alcoholic tribes, allowing herself a few glasses of wine.

But Ray could sometimes go on benders, to separate himself from bourgeois caution, live on the edge—though afterward, he might throw up for days. Sometimes it gave him a migraine, and he had to lie in bed in a dark room with a cool cloth on his head. Abby had designated an old tin pot for him to vomit in, so he wouldn't have to get up. When he barfed in it, she cleaned it and gave it back. Travel, too, gave him constant nausea, though it was years before he told her that—he thought everyone felt sick when they flew, and all Abby knew was that he turned into a jerk on planes. Once he yelled at her in front of several hundred people, because she let someone exit ahead of her, holding him up for ten seconds.

Abby sighed, a sense of failure yawning wide inside of her. She didn't want to lose Ray—she loved him, she loved his poetry. She loved taking care of him, getting him to the cardiologist, making sure he ate good food, didn't drink too much, and slept. He needed that—he had been abused, and his heart was giving out. Sometimes she felt so protective of him that he might have said the same of her, that she tried to control him, too. They were a system, fiercely focused on each other, and they always had been. In their first years, when they spent evenings with friends, she and Ray liked to squeeze together into one big chair.

"At least they're not sitting in the same chair anymore," friends noted wryly after they stopped doing that.

And these days, when they fought, it never lasted long. Just a few months before, one summer night, they had gotten in a tiff, and Ray slept in his study. But in the middle of the night, an earthquake rocked the building, and he threw back the study door and shouted, "Bean!" They ran to the kitchen doorway and stood braced, his body wrapped around hers from behind. When it stopped, both of them were trembling, and they had to crawl on all fours to their big bed, where they lay entwined.

And just, what, a month ago? When she was stressing about her paper for the MLA, and Ray was still in Providence, she sent him an email about an awful dream, in which she wrote a gory poem about partial-birth abortion and showed it to the mother of a girl who rode with her. In the dream, the woman was so upset she complained to their trainer, "because she was concerned about a person who could write such a thing." Ray wrote right back, pointing out the link to her MLA paper. He said he would be home soon and would "kiss you into better dreams, I promise." Could he have said that if he was really in love with someone else?

Enough—she just wanted to sleep. Current thinking about lupus connected it to stress, and doctors believed it never really went away, so they gave her sleeping pills and tranquillizers, a lifetime supply. Getting up, she downed an Ambien, which soon knocked her out like a death wish.

# FIVE

RAY HAD ALWAYS been able to sleep when he needed to, but tonight he couldn't stay there long, and when he woke up, it was still dark. Opening his eyelids to the blackness, he saw the familiar outline of his desk, bookshelves, and typewriter from a new angle, in ambient city light, and it gave him a sense of doom. Something wasn't right. Something was trying to get him.

He sat up quickly, looked around. But it was just the dark and quiet apartment, him exiled to the doghouse as usual. He tried to get mad—that would feel better. But the doom didn't go away.

On the bedside table, his phone glowed briefly, and he felt a twinge of fear—it would be a text from Tory, sent from Montreal, where it was three hours later than it was in Berkeley. That was what was wrong, the stake driven in his heart. He grabbed the phone and turned it off. He had to think.

He pulled on the same black jeans and T-shirt from the night before and went to the kitchen quietly, bare feet. But the door to their bedroom was closed, so Abby wouldn't hear him anyway.

In the kitchen he turned on the small light above the stove, throwing shadows over all their fucking yuppie equipment: the Cuisinart, the blender, the stand-up mixer, the ceiling rack swaying gently, hung with copper pots, the paella pan, the crab and lobster boiler, stainless-steel turkey-roasting pan, a wok, blue Le Creuset. On the walls were overloaded spice racks, a bird clock that sang different calls at each hour, the magnetic strip with fourteen knives. On shelves sat five kinds of graters, a little butter melting pot, gravy separator, ravioli press, a marble mortar and pestle. On counters, olive-wood cutting boards, French press, the Swiss burr coffee grinder, ceramic garlic pot, a vase with a bunch of fresh basil and another with wooden spoons and spatulas and ladles, a Chinese wire spoon, whisks, and a cheese plane. In drawers the melon baller, cherry pitter, lemon squeezer, turkey baster, instant-read thermometer, and several clever metal tools he had never figured out.

And on an open stretch of wall, the only sign of him in the whole room: a sampler he had made, embroidered with flowers in between the words:

❀ ❀ ❀ ❀
**GO**
❀ ❀ ❀ ❀
**FUCK**
❀ ❀ ❀ ❀
**YOUR**
❀ ❀ ❀ ❀
**SELF**
❀ ❀ ❀ ❀

It was the only thing he'd ever sewn, and usually he enjoyed the sight of it.

But today he was so anxious, his hands shook—hot decaf might help. He tried to fire up the gas burner under the kettle, and it took three tries, but he got it going finally, brushed out the beans he had ground the night before, a habit he'd developed so as not to wake Abby when he first got up.

He made coffee in the press and sat with it in the dark dining room, looking south toward Oakland at the vast expanse of city lights, strips of white fog laid over them like veils. As his coffee cooled enough to touch it with his lips, the sky showed the first sign of gray. Usually he walked to his café soon after dawn and wrote a draft of something on a yellow legal pad, in the pterodactyl scratch that was his handwriting, though even he could not always decipher it. When he wanted someone else to read it, he had to print or type.

("That is the writing of a crazy person," a friend of Abby's had once said, on catching sight of it. Yeah, yeah. Maybe he was, so what. He certainly felt that way right now.)

The walk downhill to the café was one of the high points of his day, through the cold clean salty air off of the bay, the early silence unsullied, almost no one else out of their beds. And with the time difference, he could text back and forth with Tory as he went, and no one would ever know.

But this morning something kept him home—he didn't even want to check his phone, still facedown in the study. He had thought he might feel lighter, freer now, but it was the opposite. It was like he'd lost his innocence, and texting Tory would no longer be a game, but serious, life-threatening. Maybe Johnny and Hank were right not to tell their wives. They'd just take the girl, keep mum, and any guilt was at most a pinprick in their happiness.

That was the problem here—he, Ray Stark, was turning out to be a Puritan, coming clean instead of running naked through a field of flowers with the girl. Far from being a pinprick, the guilt felt like the thick end of a wedge jammed in his chest. But Hank just wasn't right, that it was better to cheat and lie. Hank had hurt a lot of girls, and Priscilla, too, and finally himself. Ray was hurting Abby now, and God knew he felt sick, after telling her. But at least he was honest.

And what did he want next?

He could call Tory, tell her to go to Providence, into his house, and wait for him in the silk blouse.

But for some reason he didn't even want to think of her. He sat quiet, listening for the sound of Abby breathing in her sleep. She had awful dreams, and he often had to wake her up. Sometimes she even sleepwalked, dreaming with her eyes open, seeing things. Once it was a pit opening in the floor, about to suck her down. She was standing in the middle of the bedroom, making little high-pitched screaming sounds.

Another time it was a baby she had lost, and she was searching for it all over the house. He knew Abby had wanted kids, but he never did, afraid they'd be fucked up like him, or that he'd fuck them up. And Abby had mostly seemed to understand and be okay with that. She was too busy for kids anyway.

Besides, he'd never knocked up anyone—he was pretty sure that he shot blanks, though he didn't want to check. Who needed to know a thing like that? Once Abby had brought home a silly plastic cup he was supposed to jerk off into, so her doctor could check and see if they really needed birth control at all. But forget it, he wasn't doing that. He threw the cup away.

He remembered when he first saw her, in Morgantown. She had been over thirty, but she looked about nineteen, with shining blue eyes and blond curls down her back. At school she had dressed primly, to suggest professorial authority, and when he tried to talk to her at the water fountain in Colson Hall, she always skittered away. Her first-semester seminar included a week on *The Cantos*, a week on *Four Quartets*, two weeks on *Ulysses*, another on *A Vision*, then on Woolf, the Dadaists, the Futurists, Surrealists, et cetera, a reading list that was evidence of insanity. Ray almost took it anyway, just to see what she would do.

Then one night two of his friends got married, and afterward Ray went with them and another couple to Bear's, a pizza joint and bar with live music. As soon as they walked in, he spotted Abby sitting stiffly with a local celebrity—she looked extremely pretty but was clearly bored. His friends slid in a booth across the aisle, but Ray stayed on his feet, looking down at her, wondering if there was something he could do to rescue her, and she shot him a look of such longing that it sent a dart of heat to his heart. Maybe he had a chance after all.

Another English prof was a fortyish guy, divorced and hip, famous for his cooking, and he liked to hang out with grad students and junior faculty. Abby's second fall in Morgantown, the fortyish professor dug a pit, buried a whole suckling pig over hot coals, roasted it all day, and invited a big crowd.

Ray went and managed to get Abby as his partner in lawn darts. They had beaten everyone, and when the hot, succulent pig was served, with coleslaw and potato salad and beer, she sat beside him on the grass. She didn't take a paper plate, because she claimed she had to go get ready for her seminar.

Ray held his plate out to her. "Here. You have to have a taste."

And she did. She lifted shreds of tender pork right off his plate and ate them, as if they were already lovers. When she went inside to the bathroom, he waited in the hall nearby, planning to kiss her. But before she came out, other people crowded in there, and she ducked easily out of reach and slipped away.

A few weeks later, an English grad student and her husband had a party, invited some of the younger faculty, and Abby showed up in loose silk pants printed with red roses, a creamy silk blouse, and open-toed lizard-skin sandals with stiletto heels—looking, in other words, like she was tired of being remote and professorial. All the guys in the place tried to get near her, including Ray. In heels she could be slightly taller than he was, and he loved it that she was fearless about wearing them. He danced with her, mugging at his own awkwardness, the way he could only fling his limbs around.

He was pretty sure it was time to make his move, and when they stopped to drink a beer, he mentioned a poem about a flea that bites two lovers, mixing their blood.

"I've seen Blake's drawing for that poem," Abby said. "At the Tate in London."

Ray's heart pounced. "Yes, Blake did a drawing of a flea, but that was not his poem. It's by John Donne, and for that mistake I will have to kiss you."

She gave him a sweet, bemused look but did not resist—her lips were firm and smelled of roses. Johnny was there, too, saw what was happening, and he stepped close to them, turned his broad back, and raised his arms to shield them from the crowd.

When Ray stopped kissing her, Abby looked straight across at him, their eyes on the same level, and said, "Who wrote *Hamlet?*"

They had been together only a few weeks when she went west for Christmas break. She was out there for a month, and he was amazed how much he missed her. He spent hours every day on the phone with her or writing her letters, and he could hardly think of anything else. His friends got tired of hearing about her.

"Jesus, dude, she's got her hooks into you or what?" Johnny said one night, hoping to change the subject for a while.

The night she got back, he lay naked on top of her and said, "I missed you so much I started to think we should get married." Then he panicked and added fast, "Don't say anything!" which made her laugh.

They were married five months after that.

IT WAS STUPID to be sentimental now. It had been her brilliant idea to take jobs on separate coasts, and that had worn them down. Something went slack, and they'd been coasting now for years.

And lately he had realized something else, that she had always been ambivalent toward him. She could take him for only so long, just like his mom. He'd been a hyperactive kid, unable to sit still or shut up—Abby blamed his mom for hitting him, but he was pretty sure he had driven her nuts. On evenings when she'd had enough, she used to lock him in his room with a jar for pee, sometimes before the other kids even had to come inside. On summer nights, he watched them through the windows, out there playing hide-and-seek.

And Abby could get exasperated with him, too, when he was being squirrelly or talking too much about something. And she could be pretty damn dismissive about it, too. Back when she had tried to convince him about their taking jobs on separate coasts, and how they could handle that, he talked about it every night and would not be put off. Sometimes she tried to bring the discussion to a close by saying something like, "Time to hood Ray's cage," as if he were a canary that needed to settle for the night.

That memory started a slow burn in his chest, and to stop this line of thought, he put on running shoes and a down vest, got his day pack and phone and left the apartment, strode downhill toward his café. The sun was now above the Berkeley ridge, the sky clean blue, washed by rain, and he looked around, already mourning this place. New England was old and dirty, expelled from the garden long ago, and back there winter would be sinking icy fangs into trash heaps underground.

But here it was already spring, on New Year's Eve. On one slender pink magnolia tree, a bloom about the size of his head hung low, and he put his face in it. It smelled clean and fresh, and felt like baby skin.

By the time he crossed the Cal campus and got to his café, he felt better, brain newly supplied with oxygen, his face possibly pink instead of gray. The two Latino guys behind the counter greeted him, and without being told, they made his decaf latte with a pile of hot sweet foam on top. With the students mostly gone, his favorite table was available, at the end of an L up in the loft, overlooking the front door and the deadbeats sleeping on the sidewalk outside, some of them white suburban kids who gelled their hair up like the statue of liberty and begged for handouts they could get more easily from Mom and Dad.

Before he lost momentum, he sent Tory a quick text. "We can have no contact for a month. No texts, no calls, no emails. I love you, but this has to happen. Don't reply."

He pushed "Send" and sat barely breathing till his heart slowed down. A month. Thirty-one days. He'd give his marriage that clear shot. And if he still wanted Tory on January 31? Well, he did not expect that actually to go away. But at least she was out of Providence now, no longer a constant temptation. And if he never saw her again, wanting to wreck his life might end.

He took out a yellow legal pad, its top page scored with deep impressions from his ballpoint pen on the sheet above the day before, top sheet now gone, transcribed into the typewriter yesterday afternoon. It seemed good luck to use the impressed page, already half destroyed, like him, like his mind, his heart. He preferred his pens half broken, too, and always got the cheapest kind, let them stain his hands and shirts. Nothing fancy here, just like his father's dynamite and pickax in the mine, the soot he brought back on his clothes and in his lungs. He wanted his hours here in the café to leave something visible like that, blue smudges all over him.

He scribbled a few lines, the orts and scraps he had stored in his brain since yesterday. His cryptic cursive kept it private, no one able to read over his shoulder.

THE SAYINGS OF RAY-FU

Beware the new haircut.

Shirt color always lighter than pants.

Err big or not at all.

When you err big, repeat and call it jazz.

Give money whenever asked.

Don't wear that dress with that bra.

Beware any enterprise requiring new clothes.

No, wait, that's Thoreau.

Steal, then give it back, enlarged.

Climb the orchard fence, eat all you can, and leave the rest.

Keep trees on your side, and ants.

Choose wisely between crow and raven.

Never let a frog into your bed.

Know your Chinese, Choctaw, and Martian names

but keep them to yourself.

Do not disclose the source of your voodoo.

On the first day of abalone season, fourteen divers

needed rescue though they had been warned

of massive surf. Chutzpah or death wish?

The first year of marriage, you just try to figure out

what kind of death grip to put on each other.

Better to leap than look.

Better to nap than sleep.

Write all you know onto a paper airplane,

climb the tallest building you can find,

and set it free.

It seemed like he might almost get this one to fly. Blow some hot air in there, lift off and drop sandbags. Soar for a while, then gradually let hot air out like flatulence, fart, fart, drift down and fart some more, until he found a spot to perch, alight.

The balloon conceit was promising. Maybe he'd keep it around and find a way to work it in a poem of its own sometime.

Stashing tablet and pen in his pack, he slid his arms through the straps and stalked out to the Ave, as everyone called Telegraph— because, like Frank O'Hara, he needed record stores and bookstores to prove he didn't actually regret life. Restlessly he prowled down to

Amoeba and went through his favorite bins, looking for unknown discs with John Zorn or Ryuichi Sakamoto sitting in with someone else's band.

He bought two, used, crossed the street, and rifled through the stacks at Moe's to see what had come in since yesterday, found a hardly touched first edition of Ashbery, *Flow Chart*, which he of course already had, but it was too good a deal to pass up—he could give it to someone (not Tory, not Tory, not this month). One of his best guy students, Adam or Josh.

He went to the Cal gym and swam, pausing to catch his breath every few laps, like an old man. Jesus, he was such a piece of shit these days. But he made it over half a mile, took a long hot shower in the steamy, soap-smelling locker room, and dressed again.

Then it was time to face the walk home. It was all right at first, across the deserted campus, with its monumental marble buildings, Japanese tourists taking pictures of each other in the California sunshine, with the Campanile in the background or under Sather Gate. But past the Greek-temple-looking library was the first steep ramp, a forty-five degree angle, his chest on fire by the time he could see the bronze saber-toothed tiger in front of Paleontology.

There was a brief flat stretch, out the north gate of campus and across Hearst. He loitered as long as possible on the first block of Euclid, with its funky shops, some of them different each few months, only La Val's Pizza and Bongo Burger and the Seven Palms market the same from year to year.

After that, the climb was gradual for three blocks, before the awful hill began. When they had first moved here, he could run up it and often did, starting from the Cal gym, up the hill right past their place and on to the top of the ridge, hundreds of feet of elevation higher up. One day he had been running on the main road of the ridgetop, Grizzly Peak, wearing nothing but nylon shorts and a tattered tank, feeling good, springy, bounding along, when two black guys in a convertible drove up beside him and slowed, both looking at him.

"Looking tough, dude," one of them said.

Ray was thrilled but tried not to show it, just lifted his chin in acknowledgement.

Now, not quite eight years later, he almost had to crawl on all fours up the two-block rise from Hilgard to Buena Vista, his heart feeling crucified. Still blocks from home, he was so dizzy he had to stop, sit on a bench, and pant, face clammy with cold sweat, hoping the blood would make it to his brain.

# SIX

ABBY DREAMED OF her friend Gillian, that they were ice skating and laughing together, as they had done just a few years before. When she woke up, she lay in the spell of the dream awhile, wishing it was real. Gillian had been her junior colleague at Cal, and twenty years younger, but when she moved into the office next to Abby's, they became great friends and kept each other company, especially when Ray was gone.

Gill was sweet of temperament, with a quick wit, and she liked to gossip about their colleagues, how pretentious some of them could be. She was short and dark, Jewish, with a pretty face, and though she was not thin, she favored miniskirts with patterned black pantyhose, cowboy boots, and backward baseball caps. She could charm anyone, from homeless people to the department chair, who was soon taking her to lunch. Gill wrote to Abby in meetings, as if they were in junior high:

"That Renaissance guy with the big red nose? He reeks of Brussels sprouts."

"That woman is all one note, pissed off. Everyone needs more than one note."

When Abby said something she liked, Gill wrote, "You rock!" and underlined the words.

At school, Gill took care of her, brought her tea in mugs, or a turkey sandwich from the Bear's Lair. And on weekends when Ray was back east, they went to chick flicks and lounged around in front of each other's fireplaces.

Gill had left a boyfriend in New York, a German physicist, which seemed like a neurotic choice for her, and pretty soon she broke up with him for another baby English prof. That maddened the German physicist—Dieter was his name—and he called her up every night to say he was going to kill her.

"If you have a child, that child will be an orphan," he said. "If you get married, that man will be a widower."

When Abby told Ray, he tried to reassure her. "Nah, he's three thousand miles away. And guys who talk about it don't do it."

Then one spring during finals week, Abby was in her office grading papers, and Gill was in hers, with the new boyfriend down the hall. Suddenly what sounded like a bomb went off on the other side of the wall, and then more down the hall. Heavy feet ran thudding outside her door.

"Everyone, stay where you are," a man shouted. "Don't move."

Abby had crouched under her desk for hours, listening to voices cataloguing gore.

"Brain tissue," one said clearly in the next room, and she plugged her ears.

It was not until they let her out that she learned for sure that Dieter had driven all the way across the country with three guns, one of them a big Glock, which he had used to blast Gillian, her new boyfriend, and himself to kingdom come.

* * *

**TO STOP THE** memory, Abby got up, heated water for coffee, and noticed Ray's mug in the sink—the sight of it made the night before come rushing back. She started to wash it out, but it slipped and *crash*, shattered on the porcelain. When she picked up the pieces, one cut her finger, and blood welled up. She started to lift it to her mouth to suck, then stopped. Blood meant HIV! You didn't suck it off!

Of course that was absurd—she knew what was wrong with it. But she stood still, body clanging like a gong—it was as if the world had blown to pieces, and nothing was reliable. Even the day after Gillian was killed, she hadn't been this nuts.

She went over it rationally: if her blood had HIV, so did her mouth, which was unlikely, with one partner all these years. When she had the mystery illness, her white blood cells had tanked, along with her T cells. But the doctors said it was her own body attacking itself—that's what lupus was, a berserk immune system, reacting against your own DNA, like an allergy's attempt to grow up and kill people. And if she'd ever been exposed to HIV, that same ninja immune system would probably have just gobbled it up.

Of course, Ray could have gotten it from someone else and given it to her. People sometimes implied that he was too close to two women poets, who sent him little gifts, droll things they found in antique shops or made themselves. But even in love, Ray said he hadn't slept with Tory. Besides, his body's defenses were nothing compared to hers, and if he'd been exposed to HIV, he'd probably be dead by now.

She threw away the shards of mug, made coffee, and took it to her desk. It was in one corner of the bedroom, with a west window high above the bay and a view of the Golden Gate Bridge. On her laptop was another paper on *Ulysses*, but that seemed stupid now, to keep pointing out what anyone could see who read the thing. Joyce once said he "wrote to keep the professors busy," and she was tired of dancing to that tune.

She was also sick of literary theory, its insinuation that the art of any time sustains the conqueror—as if the artist meant to do that, when a person on death row will scratch frescoes on the wall with a plastic knife. Not from any hope of fame or glory, but to make something where there was nothing, to say "I was here." Best of all if you could make something beautiful. But the farmer who plows a field in particular lines is responding to a similar urge.

She refilled her fountain pen, the black and gold Montblanc Ray had given her as his first present, twenty-five years before. She took a sheet from the printer and wrote.

DEAR ROMEO

I will not be the obstacle to your romance
    the Capulet to your Montague
    the thing that makes it burn white hot, while
    you have sex with me and think of her—no thanks!
You should get closer to that belly-button ring
    that shows so fetchingly between her short-short
    cutoff jeans and midriff tank, the winged bird
    tattooed in green and blue across her butt.
Eat her cuisine of cereal and milk, the frozen pizza
    like cardboard, bottled dressing sloshed onto iceberg
    and for a gourmet reach, slices of orange cheese
    melted on top of broccoli.
Find out how she hogs the bathroom and what she does in bed
    that you can't stand.
This is an imperfect universe, as learns everyone who gets what he most wants.
In other words, please go fuck her for a while and then get back to me.

She turned on the laptop and typed it up, fooled around with the enjambment and spacing. It was far from a good poem—it was doggerel. But something about it felt just right. Poetry was a way to think, work through, make sense, and this one said exactly what she meant.

Should she print it out and leave it on Ray's desk? He might be a snob about it—it was nothing he and Johnny would admire. No, she'd keep it to herself. He'd had a secret life all these months. She could have one, too.

There was something else she needed to do now, and she went online, to social media, and searched Tory Grenier, finding several photos easily. A slender dark-haired girl, she had also posted pictures of her tall white standard poodle, Emile, along with cheerful comments in French and English containing too many exclamation points.

Wincing in advance, Abby shifted to the Brown website. Their house in Providence was not equipped with Internet, and when she was there, she had to go to the Brown library or Ray's office to keep up with her email—she used his university account and password. She had never thought to look at his email, though she could have any time. But Ray was so technically naïve, he had probably never thought of that.

Sure enough, in his inbox was a new message from Marie-Victoire Grenier, and attached to it was the entire stream, with his replies to her, going back for months. Grimly Abby hit "Print." She wasn't going to read them, but sometime she might need to, to combat her own naïveté.

As the printer spilled the pages out, she couldn't help but notice that the salutations on each message were the same: "Darling," they called each other, as if they were afraid of using the wrong name— as if he might call her Abby and she might call him Steve. In grad school, Abby had lived a thin wall away from Lorelei, a zaftig young woman with a string of lovers, whom she called exclusively "Baby," for the same reason. Often thumping sounds issued from her place along with protracted cries of "Oh, ba-a-a-a-a-by!" Lorelei had said things to her about sex, like, "Sometimes it's a banquet, and sometimes it's a picnic." Once she brought over a rotten chicken for Abby to sniff and decide if it was okay to cook. Wistfully, wanting to be anywhere but here right now, she wondered where Lorelei was today.

FINALLY RAY CAME back and walked into the bedroom. She could tell by the set of his face and shoulders that he hadn't changed his mind—he wasn't going anywhere.

"I told Tory we can't have any contact for a month."

Surprised, Abby looked at him. What was this supposed to mean, that he wanted to drag the whole thing out, torture all of them?

She didn't answer, and he walked to the kitchen. When she left her desk and went out to the dining room, he had put carrots, olives, radishes, crackers, and cheese onto a cutting board and set it on the table in the sun, as if it were any other lunch. She didn't think she could get through an hour in his company, let alone an afternoon. She wasn't going to let him give her the details. She wasn't going to help him shred a quarter century.

But for that matter, what would she do, if he left? The days ahead looked empty and hopeless. Maybe she shouldn't think too far ahead, just imagine what she could stand to do right then. On an ordinary New Year's Eve, they might drive to the coast to hike on rugged, isolated cliffs once favored by the Trailside Killer. Outside it was a piquant day, sun out after the rain, and a hike was about the only thing she could imagine doing now with Ray. So she suggested it.

They put on hiking clothes and got into the Porsche. Ray drove, with Abby navigating, because he never knew where he was going. She got them across the longest bridge, with its two peaks and the valley in between, then south to Mill Valley, with Mount Tamalpais looming green above. The Porsche zoomed up the winding mountain road, under a heartbreaking blue sky.

She kept her eyes ahead. "When you saw her in New York, did you really not sleep with her?"

"No, I swear. We only had a few hours together, walking around. We did hold hands, and I kissed her once, on the street. But that was it."

"And that's why you asked me to come with you, then told me not to, then begged me to come after all, when it was too late to get a reasonable flight. That's why you sounded panicked when you changed your mind. I should have gone. I should have gotten there for Thanksgiving."

Guiltily she remembered her relief. But no, by that time, he had already been to New York and kissed the girl.

He waved one hand as if to try to wipe away those words. "For God's sake, don't apologize. It's not your fault! I'm the weak one here. I should have never let her come."

Abby felt surprisingly calm. "Why did you let her come?"

Quickly he said, "I wanted to find out if it was real."

"If what was real?"

"The way we felt about each other."

"And was it real?"

He looked straight ahead, hands on the wheel. "I wouldn't have told you if it wasn't. It would have been just a fantasy, and I would have dealt with it by myself."

How could she still feel jealous? She should forget him right this second. It was not too late to make him drive to the airport. "Did you always want to do this? Did you just wait till you found someone who wanted you, too?"

He gripped her shoulder. "No, sweetheart, never. You were the only one for me."

"Your bad-boy buddies do it over and over."

"No, they haven't, not like this. They just go ahead and sleep around. Give me some credit here. I'm telling you about it, and I haven't slept with her. I'm trying to do the right thing. I just can't help the way I feel."

They crested the ridge and smelled the tang of the Pacific. The air was so clear they could see the Farallon Islands, barren rocks thirty miles offshore, dark silhouettes jutting out of shining blue water, home to cormorants, harbor seals, and great white sharks. The sight of them cleared Abby's head. God, she loved this place! It was her home, and in a way she must have loved it more than Ray. She had insisted on moving here, when his job was on the other coast.

On impulse she said, "I wish we lived under polygamy. I could be the senior wife."

Beside her, Ray said nothing. But he put one hand over his face.


THEY DESCENDED THE backside of the mountain, to a narrow country lane through wind-warped Monterey pines. It led to cliffs above the beach, the final miles on pale dirt road, and ended at a muddy parking lot, eucalyptus forest towering beyond.

They set off on a wide fire road, where gold light glanced off leaves that shimmered in the breeze. It was cold in the shade and warm in the sun, with puddles they had to skirt. Old eucalypti lent a hint of menthol to the air, some with girths too big for their four arms combined to reach around.

Leaving the woods, the trail skirted cliffs, white combers hundreds of feet below, blue water dazzled with sun. They walked in silence, gazing out to sea. Up the hill above them, a white-tailed kite hovered upright, white wings with black tips, white tail forming a cross, and all that beauty just stabbed Abby in the chest. A hundred times they had come here. In the old days, when they lived in Morgantown, they had spent summers in Berkeley, and always, on the day before they had to return, they came out to Point Reyes and made love on some beach, observed by seals and gulls. And now he thought he was in love with someone else?

The fire road was about to turn inland, down a ravine, and Abby stepped to the cliff's edge, the pain in her chest almost like ecstasy. She needed to stand above the long drop to the beach—it was the thing that answered how she felt. How absurd it was, the idea of lifelong marriage, when everyone changed. Ray had told her that all cells in your body were replaced every five years, including the ones in your brain. In their marriage, that had happened to each of them five times. What if there were tiny missteps in the DNA?

"Hey," Ray said, and grabbed the back of her jeans, like she might jump. He pulled her away from the edge. "What are you laughing at?"

"I was just thinking how you and I have both mutated over time. God knows, you're not the person I first met, and neither am I. I can scarcely remember who I was back then. I was terrified of speaking to more than ten students at a time. And you were getting arrested for peeing in alleyways. Now you're on CNN."

They had interviewed him once, during National Poetry Month. He had also been on NPR and the cover of *American Poetry Review*.

Devastation swept through her. How would she deal with that, seeing him everywhere, when he was gone?

She strode away, taking the trail as it curved down the ravine, toward a creek at its bottom lined with trees. She couldn't stand it. He was the person she wanted to tell whatever she thought. If she had an idea, or saw a hawk, or read something that made her laugh with surprise, she needed to share it with him—with him, and no one else. He wasn't just her husband, he was also her best friend. Marriage is conversation, Nietzsche said, and she had been in conversation with him almost half her life.

Tears slid down her face as she trudged resolutely, brushing them away. She heard him coming fast down the hill behind her, and soon he fell in next to her, matching her stride for stride. It was better than nothing, just to have him there, available to talk. There must be a way to salvage that.

"Maybe," she said. "If we really work at it, we can figure out a way to stay best friends."

Side by side they crossed a bridge over the creek, footsteps hollow on wood. Below them on both sides grew beds of cress, in water that did not appear to move.

Ray's voice came out strangled, as if his throat were tight. "Maybe, if we really work at it, we can figure out a way to stay married."

ABBY FELT REPRIEVED from a nightmare—it might not mean much, but it was something, that he'd said that. She had given him the perfect out, with implied forgiveness and a promise of friendship—and he didn't take it. He did not want out. He wanted to stay with her.

They took the trail past two big lakes, then turned onto a narrow path, where they had to edge past walls of poison oak and wade through puddles of cold water, ankle-deep. After a scramble down a sandy, eroded cliff, they reached an icy torrent that arched over a granite lip and plunged a hundred yards down to the beach.

The rocks on either side were wet with spray, but Ray leaped across and held out his long arm to her. Recklessly, she took his hand and jumped, feeling like she could fly.

And it worked—she landed fine, and soon they were sliding down beside the waterfall, through terraces of crumbling red rock, until they reached the sand.

No one else was there, except a flock of brown pelicans, resting in thin sunlight beside a creek made by the waterfall, as it carved its way down the sloping beach and disappeared into blue waves. The air was cold. But when they sat in the shelter of a driftwood log, sides of their bodies pressed together, the sun felt almost warm. All those times they had made alfresco love out here, it had been August and was usually warmer even in the fog.

Ray seemed to feel the same relief that she did. "I promise not to have any more contact with Tory."

All right, if they were going to try this, it was time to give things up, promise for good this time, to love, honor, cherish, wash out each other's puke buckets, or whatever was required.

"I can quit riding," Abby said.

Ray looked scared but shook his head. "Don't do that. You love it, and it's part of who you are now. It's a package deal, you and the horse."

Bleakness overtook her, as she stared at the ocean. "Yesterday I thought you were in love with me, but now you're in love with her. What about that?"

He watched the ocean, too, looking grim. "I can't help the way I feel, but I'll get over her. I promise you. That can't compete with us."

"What if you can't?"

He enveloped her hand in his warmer one. "That in-love feeling is crazy compelling, but you know it never lasts. We got lucky. It turned into something better for us, the only time it's ever done that for me. Or something better for me, anyway. Sometimes I wonder about you, how you feel. I think you're ambivalent about me. I think you always have been."

Well, yes, she had married him too fast, before she understood how his coal-mine manners would clash with her upbringing. And, yes, he could be controlling and angry, then the world's sweetest man—but that sort of worked for her. "You have big needs," a man once said to her, meaning that she needed too much male attention. Ray gave it to her, all right, sometimes too much and the wrong kind, and yet she stuck around. And he was the same way, hungry as a baby bird with open mouth, needing to be filled with her attention all the time.

"Aren't you toward me, too?" she asked. "You hate a lot of stuff I do. I bet nobody feels purely in love, except at first. At least we know the things we don't like about each other. And it's fun just to be with you, even after all our fights."

"Me, too," he said gruffly, and pounded her hand against his thigh. "It's fun just to go to the gas station with you."

Abby felt blasted clean by ocean air, and tired, cried out, ready to stop thinking. They stood and started back, just in time. When they reached the eucalyptus woods, the blue horizon had already swallowed the red sun, leaving a sky shading from rose to opal. They found the car and drove home in the dark.

# SEVEN

RAY MOVED HIS return flight all the way back till the night before he had to teach—Providence was only three hundred and fifty miles from Montreal, and he wasn't rushing back to temptation and loneliness. The only way to forget Tory would be with Abby right there, visible and real, reminding him of what they had. Even then, he wasn't sure, but he had to try.

He spent all the time he could with her—he talked to her as they watched movies, cooked together, held hands on the street, and made cautious, tentative love. From their apartment, he stood beside her as they watched a rare West Coast hurricane swirl across the bay, closing all three bridges. Their neighborhood went dark, all power off, but that night he built a fire in the hearth, heated the kettle over it for hot toddies, and slept beside her under a down comforter and the flannel crazy quilt she had made by hand, finishing a quilt top he had found for her in an antique store in Providence.

He tried to be nice, even after a few drinks.

But no contact with Tory made him testy, the same way it would have if he tried to give up the other pleasures he had left, like Bud Light and basketball and arguing with friends. All of it was necessary to the fragile balance of his mental health, and texting with Tory had held him together for months. Losing that was like being flayed, and he found himself barking at Abby every day.

"This is a working kitchen, not a display kitchen," he proclaimed when she brought home measuring cups in the shape of geese and wanted to leave them on the counter, in his way.

"How can you use everything in the kitchen, every time you cook?" he snapped, exasperated as he did the dishes.

"How can you leave your shoes all over the house? I trip on them everywhere."

"Do you realize there are crumbs under your desk all the time?"

But he really was trying. He even went with her to the barn, a place he hated. Just the drive out there gave him the willies. They had to go east, to the backside of the ridge, into the vast expanse of suburbs, passing under highway signs that said WALNUT CREEK— it made him want to jump out of the car. Walnut Creek was a giant mall with bloated stores, glass-encased corporate headquarters, thousands of doctors' offices and big fat houses, all set on a million acres of asphalt—a place to have babies and bore them to death. In desperation parents signed their kids up for a slew of after-school lessons, and Abby's barn was full of them, snippy little girls reeking entitlement, as strong as the smell of hay and manure.

But he was doing the right thing, and trying to be nice. So he let himself be immersed into that atmosphere, watching Abby groom her horse and ride, surrounded by wealthy women and their spoiled spawn, all on expensive mounts.

When she got off her horse, he had to ask, "How can you stand it here, surrounded by this goon squad? I bet they're all Republicans."

"Not all of them," she replied.

Imperturbably she took her horse's saddle off, groomed him again, put him back into his stall, and swept the concrete floor in front of it—the sight of which made Ray snap again. "Gee, it would be great if you ever did that at home."

It was like his mouth had been kidnapped by a teenage shit who wanted what he wanted now and didn't give a termite's ass for anything so dull as friendship, loyalty, or commitment to the person he most deeply loved.

But even knowing that didn't help. A few days after his torment at the barn, they went to a party, where a man they didn't know enthused about how wonderful it was that Abby rode. He added, "My first wife used to ride."

"Yes," Ray observed. "It is a first-wife sort of thing to do."

SOMETHING WAS EATING him, and it was not just Tory. He knew his wanting her was a symptom of something else—or something had made it possible, a vacuum of some kind. Every day that January, he walked down to the café in the early mornings and wrote, then went to the Cal gym and took a run or a swim or lifted weights. Workouts seemed to clear his head, and he had always done his best thinking then.

While he sweated, he concentrated on the thought of Abby and their marriage, and tried to be honest. It was like a mental treadmill, almost the same sequence of thoughts and memories every time, to answer the question of how it had gone wrong and what he ought to do about it now.

It hadn't only been the taking jobs on separate coasts—if it was only that, they might have survived. No, Abby had gone wrong. It started after Gillian was killed, when she cried so much Ray thought he might have to have her locked up somewhere. She told him she cried in the swimming pool, silently into the water, and on long runs. Every night after a few glasses of wine, while he watched a movie or a game, she sat beside him with an open book, and tears ran down her face.

When she did finally perk up, he was pretty sure it was because she had an affair. Soon after Gill had died, she started talking about one of her colleagues, Jacob something, a single guy, one of her new theory-spouting friends—though for him it was not Lacan, but Cixous and the rest of the French feminists. He worked on Virginia Woolf and taught feminist theory, and the chicks all ate it up with a spoon, including Abby, who sometimes had lunch with him.

Then she got a fellowship to do research at the New York Public Library, and she spent a whole semester there, while Ray was up in Providence. It was an easy train ride, and they spent long weekends together in New York, walking to museums and restaurants, having some of the best times of their life.

But it turned out Jacob was on sabbatical that semester, and where did he decide to do his Woolf research? Of course, the New York Public Library, and he rented an apartment in the village, same as them. How could Ray believe that was just a coincidence?

All that semester, Jacob was underfoot. He was short and dark and thin, a Jewish guy, with black curly hair, like Gillian—he could have been her older brother, and maybe that explained something. If Ray went down midweek, he usually found him at Abby's table in the library, or the two of them might be lunching on the steps, or strolling back from some intimate little restaurant when it was snowy out. One day when he knew the library was closed, Ray took the train down unannounced, let himself into their place, and what did he see? Jacob at their kitchen table, eating a bowl of soup. Now that was a nice little domestic scene. And was it all that had ever happened there?

"He just dropped by, and he was hungry," Abby said nervously.

Jacob looked terrified and soon got out of there.

When he was gone, Ray asked, "Does he know about my heart?"

"Of course. All my friends know about that."

Ray nodded. "He's just biding his time until I'm dead."

On the phone, Johnny said, "Of course she's bonking the dude."

Hank agreed. Both of them came to New York, sniffed around, and told Ray what they thought. She was guilty as charged.

She denied it, and claimed she often found Jacob annoying, because he liked to call her "Mrs. Stark," though she had never used Ray's name.

"It's because I say the word *husband* too often. I love it, and I say it all the time. It's music to me, like saying your name. My husband this, my husband that, I say, and Jacob thinks it's bourgeois and unfeminist. He doesn't believe in marriage. He's fathered two kids and never married anyone. I think there's something very cold in him, or cold to women anyway. He may even be gay. He's been with a lot of women, and they never stick around. Sometimes they move in with him, but soon after that, they always run for the hills."

So, all right, Ray tried to believe her—no one wants to think his wife is screwing around. And it was true that, back in Berkeley, Jacob was far less in evidence—though who knew what actually went on when Ray was out of town? He wasn't sure he could trust her anymore.

And then she went berserk in other ways. After her first horse died, she bought another, for the same price as the Porsche, and it cost so much to maintain she was buying it again, little by little, to rent its stall and buy its feed, take lessons and get it trained. Ray was sure that part of the appeal was how much time she could spend out there, out of his sight. Sure, he could see the fun in galloping over jumps, but she also had to scoop manure, and sometimes she got thrown. When she went back to riding in her fifties, she broke eleven ribs and a scapula and had her head smacked so hard she suffered three concussions, in spite of her helmet. If she had been a football player, someone would have made her stop.

He had tried to be that guy.

"No more horses," he proclaimed. "We can't afford it. It's a rich person's hobby, and we're not rich."

And when she got hurt, he threatened darkly, "If you end up in a wheelchair, I won't take care of you."

But she didn't seem to care what he said anymore. It was like she wasn't there. It was like living with a lunatic instead of his wife. Maybe a part of him had felt divorced for years, with a madwoman in his house.


OR SO IT felt to him when he was working out. That was a natural irritant, sweating so hard—something physical, and it drew his anger out.

But when he finished and stood for a long while under a hot shower, it could all float away. Then he might wonder, was it only a bad patch for Abby, another moment when he should take care of her? God knew, he'd had a few himself, and she'd been through a lot, more than he ever had. No one in his life had died, except his dad, and a cat he had in grad school. Certainly no friend of his was blown apart ten feet away. It was like she had survived a war or something, and a lethal diagnosis, too.

Of course all that left scars in her, and maybe she needed to ride, for now, as therapy—he got that. A therapist would probably cost at least that much, and he supposed he should be glad she wasn't throwing money away on that. Riding at least seemed to be surprisingly good exercise—Abby's core muscles had gotten strong and visible. When she sat on top of him, naked in bed, he teased her, counting the ones in her abdomen.

"And how many thousand bucks did this here muscle cost us, anyway?"

So, as he dried off in the locker room and dressed again, he came to more or less the same conclusion every time. He wasn't going to be the heel who left his damaged, sixty-year-old wife. Or not without putting up a damn good fight.

But halfway through the month of no contact, he felt ready to crack. Ten times a day, he wanted to call Tory, just to hear her voice, let her know he was still there. He needed something to stop him calling her. A reminder of some kind, like his wedding ring but just for this, for not leaving his wife.

So this time he didn't ask Abby. He went to a tattoo parlor on Telegraph and let them prick him a thousand times, the pain his penance. He drew the design himself, chain links around one wrist, and on the tender underside, a tiny red padlock. It was something he could cover with his cuffs and keep secret, like self-inflicted stripes across his back.

When Abby caught a glimpse of it that night, still raw and bleeding, she looked aghast. "Good God, what's that? A tattoo? Why?"

"To remind me of how I have fucked up my life."

She peered at it. "But chains? Is that what you feel like, that you're in chains because of me? You're not in chains, you're free. I told you to go be with her!"

She seemed overwrought, but there was nothing to discuss. He'd done it, and it was now part of him. He gently washed the wound and put on an old pair of soft, well-worn PJs, in case it bled. In bed, he left the wrist exposed, so it could ooze and breathe. It stung like hell, but he deserved it. If he could have crucified himself, he might have gone with that. He concentrated his whole mind on it.

ON JANUARY 20, the tattoo was not quite healed, but it was time for him to fly back and teach, and only eleven days till the month was up. It was a chore, flying in winter, with hours of delay at every connection due to snow, and it took all day to get to Providence.

That was all right—he dreaded being there, so relatively close to Tory, though she might not be in Montreal right then. Last time he talked to her, she had made plans to spend time soon—he wasn't sure exactly when—above the Arctic Circle, cross-country skiing with friends. It sounded slightly insane, like something he might have done when he was her age.

When he reached his little house, he discovered that the pipes were frozen, and he had no water. Cheered by the emergency, he called a plumber, who couldn't come for the next two days. So he took his biggest pots and went back and forth to the yard to scoop up clean snow and heat it on the stove. It felt good to work hard in the cold, breathing icy air. More penance, more distraction, keeping him on course.

He taught the first two weeks of classes, met his new crop of scared little geniuses, before he heard from Miami. But finally he got the call, asking him to fly down for two days, to meet the deans and teach a class in front of the whole English Department.

Next morning, he walked over to the department office and in on Whitney Ames, who as usual looked fat and misbuttoned, sitting at his cluttered desk in a sloppy cardigan. He looked so stupid, slack-jawed, breathing through his mouth, and he never seemed able to focus on anything Ray said—he tended just to drop papers, with a vague look in his eye that screamed, *I am incapable, how did I get this job?* Once Ray saw him asleep on a couch in the faculty lounge, abandoning all dignity. When Ray made an appointment with him, there was always a fifty-fifty chance Whitney would forget. So this time, he just walked in.

He knocked on Whitney's desk to wake him up. "I'm going to miss a class next week. I'll be out of town."

"What for?" Whitney asked suspiciously.

The piece of shit. But he did seem to pay attention now.

"I have a flyback for the endowed chair at Miami. I'm going to take it if you don't give me a full-time job."

"Oh, really," Whitney said, not like a question, more a flat statement, or like he was trying ineptly to make fun of Ray. Whitney looked nervous, and he fumbled with a pencil till he dropped it.

That felt good, excellent, as Ray left the office and walked back home. It was a cold sun-out morning, crisp, with cardinal chatter in the air and ice windows on the puddles he could break. Spring felt thirty paces off—he could feel it polishing its helmet, buffing the fender of its equipage. For a nanosecond the head of Wallace Stevens seemed to appear in Ray's own frosty breath, and thank God he hadn't put him on the syllabus of his seminar. Next time he would call the class Abundance, and there Stevens would be, white and photosensitive but with a poetics of cockatoos.

As the time approached to fly to Florida, he ironed a few clean shirts, picked what he'd wear, the calculated look that said "Poet, but Civilized," conversant with academe. That included a few neckties, but nothing old-school—he had a Miró print on one, a surreal Italian abstract on another. Black jeans, rubber-soled black walking shoes, and which jacket? It would be warm down there—he pulled out one Abby had bought for him some years ago, unconstructed black linen, high-end, though by this time it was baggy and respectably beat-up. He could play the game, but he was also his own man.

That night he was about to switch off his phone, when it *pinged* for a text. His heart leaped—but he told himself it was probably just Abby, just his wife.

It wasn't. The screen said, *New Message from Tory Grenier.*

He started to shake. What was she trying to do?

Quickly he checked his calendar—ah. It was February now. He touched the message, and it sprang to life.

Only two words, in a gray bubble. "Snow fox."

# EIGHT

VALENTINE'S DAY MORNING, Abby dreamed that Gillian lay in a coffin, as a stylist combed her hair into ringlets. Her face was just as it had been in life, lovely, smooth-skinned, and young, just a little plump, with a heart-shaped mouth and vulnerable eyes.

*Oh, thank God, her face wasn't hit!* Abby thought with joy.

Then she herself was in the coffin, and it had a little window in the top. Ray looked into it and called to Johnny, "Come see how cute she looks in there!"

She woke up and had to lie in bed for a long while, putting the world together the way it really went. She knew the dream was wishful, but she tried to keep the feeling. Somewhere, in some other universe, Gillian was still herself, intact. Abby sometimes felt her presence. At the MLA Convention, when she was about to read her paper to a packed hotel ballroom, she had lifted her hand and felt Gillian's reach down to grasp it.

Dreamily, still half asleep, she remembered one of the last evenings she had spent with her. It was late at night, after a movie, as they sat in Gill's living room, Gill on the couch with her cat, Abby in a chair a few yards away. Abby was about to leave when Gillian gave her a long sultry look and said, "You know, I've dated girls some, too."

She wore dark red lipstick on her luscious mouth, and just for a moment Abby had considered what it would be like to kiss those lips. Certainly she loved her enough for that. But she let the moment pass, went home, and two weeks later, Gillian was dead.

IT HAD BEEN almost five years now, and these days she could sometimes think of her without crying. But it was better not to dwell.

So she got up and made coffee, read the notes for her survey class. It was a big lecture, and she had to use a microphone—she dreaded it, all those students arrayed up the slope in front of her, waving like palm trees in the breeze. Her aim would be to make them all stop moving at once, by saying something startling, or getting a laugh—which was relatively easy, since they were a captive audience. She picked out a wool skirt and high-collared blouse, stockings and heels, her power clothes.

She was about to drive downhill when she heard the hollow rumble of a UPS van out front, bringing a package from Ray. Inside was a US Navy sailor's jumper that looked barely big enough for her, and a hand-printed note.

*Got this in the same store as our quilt top. Real WWII Navy— those fellows were small. Cold, cold morning, me about to trudge forth into the white heap of Saturday, squirrels humping through the snow, beating their diagonals to the feeder for what I've spilled*

*and the cardinals kicked out. If you were here we could just get*
*back into bed. I would hate to leave this house but if we keep it,*
*we definitely need to do some things to make it snugger, new doors*
*and windows will be big, maybe a couple big rugs—it'll be fun,*
*or we'll be getting some place in Miami with gators in the yard.*
*Florida daffodils? Why not, and certainly wisteria. I'm ready*
*though to get out of the blender, for us to concentrate on being*
*together and knowing where that will be. I'm pretty much sure if*
*I get the offer, I go, don't think the mouth breather and a brick*
*wall are capable of getting an appropriate response together. Part*
*of me hopes nothing happens in a way, just to avoid the crisis and*
*the rejection I won't be able to help but feel from here. Oh well, I*
*don't know how much I can prepare for that—just try to put myself*
*together for this week's trip, which I think could be kind of fun, I'll*
*certainly be in the center ring of the circus there for a bit. Clown?*
*Lion tamer? Acrobat? I guess it's my pick and I'll try to be all of*
*them. I miss you, String Bean. I do so so love you you you*

*Ray*

She checked her calendar—just as she thought, it was his day to
fly to Miami.

By the time she finished her lecture, he had texted her from both
airports, and that night he called from his hotel, cranked up. He'd
had lunch, cocktails, and dinner with his potential colleagues and
deans, and he'd been talking fast all day. He couldn't seem to slow
down now, though it was after ten in Florida.

Almost chattering, he said, "It's a new position, donated by this
visionary guy, to start a program in experimental poetry, and I'd get
to design it. I'd only have to work with grad students, people I could

pick. So it doesn't sound so bad, with the money and all. Do you realize what kind of bucks we'll have if I come here? We could buy a house. The English Department's big. They said they could probably offer you something, too. Oh, yeah, and the dean's wife rides. He said there are excellent stables around."

"Sounds like they want you," Abby said.

"The chair told me I was in. Not that I want to leave Brown."

"Well, wait till you get the letter, then tell Whitney Ames."

"That fucking mouth breather. I did send him an email asking for a meeting with the heavies in the program."

A week later, back in Providence, he got the formal offer from Miami, and he called her. "I decided to push as far as I could. I asked for a bigger salary, and they agreed like it was nothing." He giggled. "Oh, and they mentioned a job for you again. We could live together all the time. Of course we'd keep the Berkeley place for summers. So think about it, okay?"

THE DAY OF his meeting with the senior faculty at Brown, they texted back and forth from the time Abby woke up. When he didn't write back for a while, she knew it must be happening.

Ray's ring on her phone was ducks quacking, and finally she heard them.

"Fucking mouth breather wouldn't know an idea if it bit him on the ass. And Gumby just licks his boots and swallows hard." Gumby was what he and Hank called another of their colleagues, a pudgy guy who always agreed with Ames. "Wags his fat tail the whole time. One of these days I'm going to get a gun and blow them all away."

"Please, honey," Abby said. "Take a deep breath. You might have to work there for the rest of your life. Better practice putting up with them."

"I'm tied in knots. Hank says it's in the bag, but I don't think he's right."

She thought about it for a while. "You know, you hate those people. You might still want to walk away. But it should be your choice. So please, try to tread cautiously until it's figured out."

He had to answer Miami in ten days, and Brown promised to let him know by then. When the time was almost up, Abby flew to Providence, where it was deep winter. She made beef stew and listened to Ray fret, to her and on the phone with Hank and Johnny. He seemed too tense to sleep, and the second night she was there, she woke at 3:00 A.M. to find him upright downstairs on the couch, fiddling with his phone. He gave her a furtive look.

"What's going on?" she asked.

"Nothing. You were flopping around, and you woke me up."

"Oh, I'm sorry."

Abby felt guilty. Since New Year's, she had been so anxious she had taken Ambien every night, and it seemed to make her restless in her sleep. She knew she ought to stop, but she just couldn't right now, the way things were with Ray. Though she still refused to believe she'd had lupus, her doctors said it could come back any time she was under stress, and that a full night's sleep was the best defense—especially in spring, when it was most likely to kill a person. Quietly she went back upstairs to bed.

ABBY HAD GONE to grad school with a woman named Clarice, who was now a well-known poet and a colleague of Ray's at Brown. When Clarice found out Abby was in Providence, she called and said, "We need to talk."

They arranged to meet at a little soup and sandwich place, and Abby dressed for it warily. Clarice was a loyal friend, but she had a tendency to mother people and give unwanted advice. Had she found out what was going on with her and Ray? She was married to his mentor, Walt, and he and Ray did talk sometimes. Abby put on jeans and a cashmere turtleneck, snow boots, and a down vest that turned out not quite warm enough for the icy day outside, so she walked fast to the lunch spot.

Clarice was from New York, and she arrived bundled in an ankle-length down coat that dwarfed her small frame, a close-fitting knit cap, and a series of wool scarves. It was overheated and steamy in the restaurant, and as Abby gradually warmed up, Clarice unwound her scarves, used one to rub the steam from her wire-frame glasses, and finally pulled off her cap, releasing long straight hair, the red of which changed shade every time they met. Today it seemed to have cotton-candy highlights and beet undertones.

"God, this hair. It gets all staticky in wintertime." She tried to smooth it down.

As soon as they had ordered, Clarice wasted no time. "So, listen. I have to talk to you about Ray. What's up with him? I heard him yelling in the office the other day."

Abby was alarmed. "In the office? His office?"

Clarice stared at her without blinking, skillfully applied mascara fringing her brown eyes. "No, that was what was strange. He was in the department office, yelling at Janet." She glanced around and dropped her voice. "Nobody yells at Janet."

Janet was the departmental administrator, popular with faculty and students.

Clarice shook her head. "I don't think anyone ever has, and if they did, they wouldn't get away with it. Whitney is very protective of her."

"Was Whitney there?"

"No, but I'm sure he heard about it. All the secretaries heard, and Ray called him a mouth breather, just like that, in front of everyone! It wasn't a good move."

"Could you tell what it was about?"

"Something to do with one of his students. But he doesn't seem to need a reason. He gets mad now in every meeting. That's not going to do him any good around here."

Abby tried to make light of it. "He's under a lot of pressure, what with having to decide about Miami, and I think his heart is getting worse. He's in pain all the time, in his chest, and no one seems to know why, though it obviously has to do with his heart."

Clarice gave a little worried nod. "I wonder if his brain is getting enough oxygen, because of the weak heart. Doesn't it seem like his personality has changed?"

Abby had thought that herself, but she wasn't going to say so to Clarice, who presumably would get to vote on Ray going full time.

When the soup arrived, she changed the subject to their work, and they talked about the poetics study Clarice was trying to write and how bored Abby had become with Joyce studies. They decided they should change places, teach each other's classes for a while.

Two days later, Abby flew back to Berkeley, and next morning, Ray called. "This is it. The mouth breather wants to see me. Wish me luck."

An hour later, he called back, shouting. "He fucking fired me! He can't do that. He isn't even qualified to hold that job. He doesn't have the chops, and he knows it. And I do! Half the students here come to work with me. How many come to work with him?"

"What? Wait," Abby said. "He can't fire you. You have a contract. No, you have tenure. You have tenure at half time."

"Well, he did. He told me to take the Miami job."

"But he didn't fire you. He can't fire you."

"Quit saying that! It's the same thing. I can't stay here, not after that. And fucking Hank—I could kill him. He knew about it, and he didn't stop it. I'll never speak to the two-faced jerk again. And now I have to fucking go to Florida."

"You sure? You could still stay at Brown. What's changed, really?"

"I'd rather kill myself, and all of them," he said.

"Poet goes postal," Abby said. But today she couldn't make him laugh.


RAY SAID YES to Miami, and Abby flew back to Rhode Island and put their house on the market, both of them sad to see it go.

"I fucking cry every time I swim, the same as you," he told her bitterly.

She hadn't realized it, but they both must have counted on Brown to come through in the end. And she had misgivings about the move. Could they really live in Florida? She knew nothing about the place, except that it was full of retirees in high-rises along the beach, and former Cubans angry at Castro. There was that corrupt election with the hanging chads, and megachurches that sent people out to attack Planned Parenthood. But she had seen a photo in a riding magazine of a house somewhere down there, with an outdoor living room on grass, and a horse with its head over one couch, having its ears stroked. She would cling to that.

Ray flew to Berkeley for spring break, seeming tense but subdued.

A few nights later, their friends Sateesh and Gloria came over for dinner, as they often did, the couples dining back and forth. Sateesh was a tall, thin poet with a mane of shaggy black curls, who often wrote about his immigrant family. He had gone to grad school with Abby, written a dissertation on the literature of the Indian diaspora, and might have taken an academic post. But instead he married Gloria, blond heiress to a Chicago trucking dynasty, and neither of them had to work. Now Sateesh read widely, wrote poems, and designed software for fun. Gloria spent most days riding her three horses, and Abby suspected her of being a Republican, though when they met, they talked horses instead of politics. Gloria was plump, with a formidable bosom, large pale eyes, and graying hair kept bobbed and restrained in a ponytail. She liked to refer to herself in the third person, as in, "Nine thirty is when Gloria gets up," and, "Gloria needs a cheeseburger for lunch." Once she had nursed Abby through the flu when Ray was out of town.

Tonight, when Sateesh saw Abby, he cried joyfully, "Look how she's dressed!" Gloria shot him a glance, like he should stop, but he went on. "Look at her!"

Abby blushed—what was so unusual? It was true, she was dressed in Gloria's style tonight, flats and narrow pants with a silk tunic. Did that mean Gloria disapproved of her usual weekend wear? Too young, too sexy, she supposed. Too un-Republican. At home she and Ray still dressed the way they always had, since their respective college days—hers in the late sixties, his in the seventies—jeans and cotton sweaters, Ray in running shoes, Abby in wedge-heeled espadrilles. Some of their clothes were literally from college days, a few sweaters at least.

But now it seemed that Gloria had embraced her middle age and was critical of Abby for not doing so—and not of Ray? No, Sateesh and Gloria adored Ray, always had. She could hear the different tone in their voices when they talked to him. "Darling Ray," Gloria called him.

Well, Abby was not uncritical of Gloria, who flatly refused to have dinner with some of their other friends, academics who talked over her head. But Ray was deeply loyal to both Sateesh and Gloria and never offered to murder them—probably because they adulated him. They listened respectfully and never argued back when he held forth—they almost took notes. Abby supposed that was Ray's model of ideal friendship, at which Johnny and Hank—and she herself—had often failed.

Then, too, she supposed their preference for Ray might be based on class. Despite their current wealth, Sateesh and Gloria had roots in the proletariat, like Ray. Sateesh's father had stowed away from Mumbai rupeeless, worked the docks in New York, made foreman, and sent Sateesh to MIT to become an engineer, though he had veered instead toward books and poetry. Gloria's grandfather had won his first truck in a poker game and eventually founded his own company.

Well, that's how money was made in America. And yet, even in a supposedly classless society, it mattered how many generations you were removed from honest sweat, since someone could resent you over it. Abby's forebears had been scruffy pirates in the Gold Rush, but now they'd gone to college for a century, and all her life, people had said of her, "Thinks she's better than the rest of us." Her first semester as a professor, when she had felt profoundly like a fraud, some kid wrote on his evaluation, "Thinks she's God, but I see no connection." Whatever gave him that impression might be what put off Sateesh and Gloria.

Ray liked to cook with other people there, relegating Abby to the sous chef role, and tonight he produced a paella of chorizo and shellfish, while Abby made a salad of sugar snap peas and pocket arugula, with basil and burrata. Their kitchen was small, but they moved easily around in it, one of them washing something at the sink while the other chopped or stirred, trading places, never getting in each other's way, while Sateesh and Gloria sat on stools at the bar, tasting the wine they'd brought.

"I love watching you two cook together," said Sateesh. "It's like ballet."

Abby and Ray glanced at each other and smiled, and the mood of the night seemed saved.

The paella was excellent, and as usual the four of them sat for a long time at the table afterward, drinking wine and telling stories in the candlelight. Gloria had brought dope, and Ray rolled a joint and smoked it with her. Sateesh preferred wine, and Abby had never liked marijuana, not even in college, when it was in style. And what was available these days was just too strong—the one hit she had taken the past few years had made her giddy for fifteen minutes and then useless for a day.

Gloria seemed giddy, too, once the joint was smoked, and she could not seem to stop talking, about her mother in a mansion on the Chicago North Shore, how difficult she was, how stingy, how none of her siblings spoke to her anymore and she, Gloria, had to shoulder the burden by herself.

"Gloria," Sateesh said sternly several times, trying to make her stop. But the dope made her impervious, and after a while he gave up, stood, and commanded her to come with him, though he practically had to carry her out the door.

"Poor Gloria," Abby said, elated by comparison—Ray tried to control her only when they were alone. With others there, he seemed especially loving and often bragged of her supposed accomplishments.

Dope cranked Ray up, too, not so much to talk as to want to have fun. When he smoked, he might bounce on the bed at 3:00 A.M. and say, "Let's do something!"

Tonight he put on Frank Sinatra and asked Abby to dance. The living room was dark, lit only by streetlight outside, and in the shadows they danced slow to "Strangers in the Night," "It Was a Very Good Year," and "When Somebody Loves You," and twirled to "New York, New York," until Ray was finally tired enough to sleep.

NEXT MORNING, SHE didn't have to teach, and when Ray walked to his café, she sat at her desk, facing her big bay view. It was a beautiful spring day, rain chasing sun. Fluffy white clouds soared, their shadows darkening the blue water. She wrote another surreptitious poem, about Ray and marriage, called "The Emergency Was Over."

After an hour on that, she decided to tackle the monthly bills—the one for their phones was larger than usual. Somehow, in February, they had used more data than their family plan allowed.

Online, she clicked a link to the details and found about six hundred texts from Ray's phone, some to herself, but most to a number she didn't recognize—four of them that morning before she woke up.

Quaking like an eight on the Richter scale, she called his cell. "Have you been texting Tory Grenier?"

"I'm coming home right now to talk about it," he said in a monotone, and hung up.

Abby typed in the number from the data-usage file.

"Get your thumbs off my husband," she wrote, and pressed "Send."

Things she had been trying not to see washed over her. In January, she had spoken at a memorial for one of her Cal mentors, with Ray in the audience. It went on for three hours, and afterward, at the reception, he had oddly declined a drink and said he needed air. He went outside on the Cal campus for half an hour and came back all sparkly eyed. He had taken his phone with him, but she did not question it.

She pawed through the calendar—the memorial had been January 19. Did he call Tory and say he couldn't bear a month with no contact?

The apartment door burst open, and Ray rushed in. "Did you text her? Jesus, you freaked her out. 'Does your wife know my number?' she wrote to me."

Abby tried not to shout. "And I'm supposed to worry about her feelings? You've sent her four hundred messages in the past month. You said you were going to have no more contact with her. You've been lying to me!"

Face pale, he collapsed onto the bed. "I did not lie. I said I would have no contact with her for a month, and that's what I did."

"You've heard of lies of omission? You didn't tell me you were back in touch. And emails, too, I bet, all of it white hot, as only Romeo and Juliet can be, separated by the ogre wife. Please, now will you go sleep with her? That's how to find out if it's real. Sleep with her, wake up with her, see what she's really like. There's nothing the slightest bit real about what you're doing now."

"Jesus, Abby, it's only texts. I need time to work through it."

"Four hundred messages is working through it?"

He looked at her grimly. "I told you I was in love with her. I've been going through hell over it, on top of all the shit at Brown. It takes time." He closed his mouth in a straight determined line and just gazed at her for a while. "And I am going to McGill in April. I'll see her one last time."

Abby felt like she might faint. She knew he had been invited to read in Montreal, but she thought he had canceled it, because Tory was there. Speechless, she stared at him.

He sighed. "I know. But it's just professional. I won't see her alone. She's coming with several of her friends."

When she still said nothing, he rubbed his face with both hands. "Bean, I'm doing my best. I want to stay with you. But you have to let me work through this my way."


**WHEN HE FLEW** back to Providence, Abby lived in dread, powerless to stop his trip to Montreal. Had she ever had any influence on him? If she had, it was now stretched too thin, with the distance between their jobs. She didn't think she could ever get it back.

And yet Ray called her every night and sent her texts all day. When it was time for him to go to Canada, they texted back and forth. That night, after the reading, he called her late, half asleep in his hotel room, and said it all went fine.

"Was Tory there?"

"Yes," he said tensely.

"Did you talk to her?"

"In a group, with her friends. But I will see her alone tomorrow for an hour. It'll be the last time. I owe her that."

Abby wanted to reach through the phone and wring his neck. Had he planned that innocent hour all along?

"For what? She tried to end our marriage. Tell her thanks a million and get lost!"

"Easy, Bean. She'll drive me to the airport and that'll be it. I won't see her again."

There was nothing she could do. She needed to prepare for class, and she could not sit still. Reading as she paced the living room, she was too miserable to take much in. Finally she set the alarm for 6:00 A.M., took a Xanax and an Ambien, and washed them down with vodka, hoping for oblivion.

# NINE

**THE NEXT NIGHT,** when Ray got back to his house in Providence, he barely had the strength to stick his key into the lock and turn. He felt sick, his whole body in pain, not just his chest—he was used to pain around the heart, but this radiated out to all his veins. Saying good-bye to Tory at the airport felt like the hardest thing he'd ever done. She had cried as he held her, her sweet-smelling, silky hair against his lips. He had not been able to say he would never see her again.

"I know it's not the end," he had said fiercely. "It's not the end. I have to see you again."

Jesus Christ, did other men go through this kind of shit, to stay married? Was that how it was done? It was exhausting to think about, the amount of pain smeared across the landscape, men staggering like zombies, stricken to their kidneys, the image of some girl engraved onto their hearts. It was bad enough when you just wanted them, and they were oblivious to you. But when they loved you back? Man, that could kill a guy stronger than him.

In his mailbox was a postcard from Johnny, made from the cover of Ray's latest book, *Death Ranger*, modified to read *Death Deranger*. Collaged onto it was a photo of Ray with a demented grin and a subtitle, *New and Selected Tantrums*. That was probably because of an argument they'd had lately through the mail, Johnny maintaining that language could and should refer to things and not go off ravening across the landscape, ripping up trees and spawning new life-forms, the way Ray liked. On the back of the postcard, Johnny wrote, *You should listen to your friend Johnny, not yourself.*

Well, thank God for Johnny, even if he insisted on lining himself up with the most boring bourgeois pundits. He was good for a laugh anyway. And Ray seriously needed a laugh right then.

He called Abby, gave her a terse report, then drank five beers, staring miserably at basketball on his small TV, hoping the alcohol would knock him out. It didn't. He wished he could have the next few months surgically removed, so he wouldn't have to go through them, the withdrawal cold turkey from love—Why cold turkey? Better cold octopus, cold clam, cold platypus—withdrawal cold platypus from love. But the sooner he got it over with, the sooner he could start recovering. Time to rip it out.

At 3:00 AM, tears running down his face, chest throbbing, he started on his sixth beer. Who cared? He couldn't help himself— he had to say something to Tory, one last time. Just one more text.

"My dearest, only darling," he wrote. "I will love you forever, and you had better love me, too, forever and ever, you got that? With all your heart. But it has to be the end. It has to be. It can't go on. I love you with my bone marrow, my spleen, my toenails, but it has to be the end. I'm sorry."

Weeping harder, he pressed "Send."

Half a minute later, his phone lit up, making cricket chirps—Abby's ring. What was she doing up, at midnight in Berkeley? He answered it.

She sounded alarmed. "Was that a suicide note?"

Panic lashed him. "Was what a suicide note?"

"You said you would love me forever and I had to love you, too, but it had to be the end. You said you can't go on."

Ray tried to speak and had no voice. He cleared his throat. What the hell had he just done? On his phone were messages from Tory but also from his wife, right next to each other, because he often wrote them both at almost the same time. His clumsy finger must have tapped on the wrong one, before he started to write.

"My God. That was not for you. That was for Tory."

Her voice hit a high C. "You love her with your bone marrow, your spleen, your toenails? You're going to love her forever? What do I have to do to make this stop, kill myself? For God's sake, go be with her. I'm done. Good-bye!"

She hung up, and Ray immediately called her back. Had she just said she was going to kill herself?

He listened to her phone ringing. On his end it sounded like an old-fashioned ring—but not on hers. On hers, it would be that absurd and hateful duck quacking. Was she laughing at him, setting it like that? The call went to voicemail, and he hung up, called back. *Quack quack quack.*

For an hour, he continuously tried her phone. He wanted to scream, fling his through the glass French doors that led nowhere, just to two uncomfortable, overlong steps down to a cracked patio and bare brown lawn, traumatized by winter and not yet spring, like a scene from hell. In Berkeley it would all be green and blooming by this time, roses and wisteria spilling over trellises, mock orange trees half drowning you in cloying sweet scent as you passed.

Why was he here, in a place where no one wanted him? What had he done to deserve this exile from his life, so far away he could not stop his wife from whatever she might do? Pills, probably—she had a deep stash. The last few months, she had been hooked on Ambien, and after she took it, she would fall asleep and then get up and walk around, doing and saying things she would not recall in the morning. The bottle said not to drink on it, but of course she did. She scoffed hubristically at labels that said not to, as if getting past the lupus made her a medical expert.

It actually crossed his mind to call the cops, which was insane, after the nights he'd spent in the drunk tank in Morgantown, when he had nothing to lose, and he was a guy. Abby was too vulnerable, both as a professor with a reputation to protect and a chick who could be hurt in ways they'd never try with him. But, good God, he had to do something.

It was almost one o'clock in Berkeley, but the hell with that. Their downstairs neighbors seldom seemed to sleep, lights blazing in their place all night. He called them, but they did not pick up.

So he called Joel, their friend across the hall. Joel was a divorced, aging historian, expert on intellectual trends in France, and a very measured guy, who had never done anything impulsive in his life. He kept his white hair trimmed precisely at three-quarters of an inch and never looked as if he'd had it cut. He worried about the correct attire for any occasion, what restaurants were trendy and which passé, and if drinking wheatgrass was still in fashion with the young? He was not asleep, and Ray asked him to please go check on Abby.

"Our key's in the lockbox if you need it," Ray reminded him. The lockbox was in the basement, and all the owners' keys were in there, and they all had keys to open it in emergencies.

When Joel didn't call back right away, Ray almost went insane.

Finally his phone rang. Joel sounded nervous, like he could not decide the proper way to negotiate such a call.

"Uh, Ray? I'm sorry to have to tell you, but I found Abby lying in the hall right outside my door, looking like she'd been beaten up. She was moaning, and I couldn't rouse her. So I called 911. The ambulance just left."

Ray felt the blood drain from his brain—he almost passed out. "Where have they taken her? Is she all right?"

"Well, she had this ugly purple bump on her cheekbone, like she'd slammed it into something. A hematoma, I guess you'd call it, like a big black knob. Black eyes, too, I'm guessing, by this time. The most disturbing thing was—"

Joel stopped, as if embarrassed to go on.

"What?!" Ray demanded.

"Well, it's just that she was in her nightgown, and it's kind of sheer, and they wouldn't get her a robe. I asked them to go into your place and get one, but they said, 'We take them as they are.'"

Ray couldn't stand it. Abby had always worn these thin cotton gowns, white or pale blue, made of something called batiste, like for a little kid. And now she'd been hauled off like that and manhandled by a bunch of firemen and EMTs? And the lump on her head—how did she get that? What was she doing in the hall?

He called the nearest hospital in Berkeley, but they wouldn't tell him anything—maybe they didn't have her yet. He waited half an hour and called again, but they didn't recognize her name. Was she still out cold and couldn't tell them? The place was incompetent—he and Abby knew two women whose husbands had died there unexpectedly, after botched surgeries. The summer before, Abby had spent two days there in the CCU, after a concussion when her horse threw her—though it wasn't her head they were interested in. They had decided she had an ectopic pregnancy, when she was almost sixty—they wouldn't stop giving her tests for it, and they kept her passive with a morphine drip. Finally Abby had asked Ray to take out her IV and go demand her clothes. As they walked out together, her doctor had protested that she had not been released. But the next day, she was fine.

Every hour now, he called the ER there, still no luck, as the sky got light in Providence. Finally it occurred to him that, if they wouldn't fetch her robe, they also didn't get her purse, so they probably had no idea who she was—if she was there at all. He called all the other hospitals in the East Bay, but no one was treating her. What if she had run away from them and made it to a bridge somehow and jumped? Or got mugged on the way? He called her cell phone for the hundredth time.

Ravaged from lack of sleep, he felt something yawning in his solar plexus.

Trying to distract himself, he walked through the cold spring morning to his Providence café, got a decaf latte, and pulled out an article he had clipped from the San Francisco paper, about a super-massive black hole that had lately been confirmed by X-ray observations on satellites.

He put it into lines to start a poem:

> Scientists concluded that the telescopes had witnessed
> the overpowering gravity of a black hole

as it tore apart a star and gobbled up a hearty
share of its gaseous mass. It was an act of stellar
mayhem known as a stellar tidal disruption.
It removed any lingering doubt that the reputation of black
holes as star destroyers was fully deserved.
The most awesome black holes, with densely packed
masses equivalent to millions or billions of suns,
are found at galactic cores. This one is estimated
to have a mass of about 100 million suns.
Don't look at me like that.
My wife has killed herself.

Nothing else attached itself to that—he felt too sick to go on, even without that last line. Space always made him queasy, with that view of the blue marble glowing in black emptiness, black nothing without end.

And what was a black hole but death, in its most violent form? And that was the core of every galaxy, the big black hole of death. Black holes had swallowed ninety billion humans in the past, and now they salivated for the rest of them, to suck them in, not only their lives and bodies but their minds, their thoughts and loves, every good thing. Like his marriage. Like his beloved Abby, who might already have been vaporized in one.

How could people stand it who did not believe in God? Not the patriarch of Genesis, no, some guy spying on them from his throne and counting his time in days. But what about this infinity of species, all this consciousness and beauty, springing out of nothing on this rock, in just a couple of hundred million years? How could you think it did that by itself?

Abby would say: "Spina bifida. HIV. Crib death. The guinea worm. What kind of god would allow all that? It's only bearable if it's just chance and no one's fault."

That rock-bottom atheism seemed to sustain her somehow. But if that was all he had, he would go nuts. He was too aware of exploding stars and the billion galaxies you couldn't even see. And when one hypothesis went belly-up, it didn't mean the question was wrong. Only the answer you found. You had to try again.

He put away his notebook—he'd come back to that on another, better day, to black holes and God and atheists, the one blue shining planet in the sky, and his beautiful wife. Just not today.

SOMEHOW, THAT AFTERNOON, he had to lead a graduate workshop. He got himself to class but could barely speak, he had so little life-force left. On the break, he called Abby, but she did not pick up.

After workshop, he dragged his body home, lay on the bed with an arm over his eyes as the early dark came down.

He tried Abby again, and this time he shouted onto her voice-mail. "How can you be so fucking irresponsible not to call and let me know you're okay? You don't have one shred of decency! You say you're going to kill yourself, and then you get dead drunk, knock yourself out, and get taken off in an ambulance, and you don't fucking let me know that you're not dead?"

Finally his phone rang.

"I wasn't drunk," Abby said calmly. "I didn't even have a hangover today. I just OD'd on tranquillizers and sleeping pills. I kept taking more, trying to feel better and calm down, but I ended up taking too much. I have a bruise on my cheek, and a black eye, but that's it."

"And where the fuck have you been all day? Why haven't you called me?"

"I had a jumping lesson this morning. It was a good ride. And then I had to teach."

He wanted to scream. "You went to the barn and rode instead of calling me to say that you weren't dead? What the hell were you thinking?"

"Because I was through with you, of course. How dumb do you think I am? You told your girlfriend you would always love her and she was your only darling. That was a love letter posing as a breakup note. And I didn't say I was going to kill myself. I said something stupid like 'What do I have to do to make this stop, kill myself?' Maybe there's a threat in that, but it's not very direct. And Joel did call this morning to see if I was okay. You could have found that out from him. Thanks a lot, by the way, for getting him involved and invading my privacy."

Ray was breathing too hard to answer for a minute. "I will not apologize for trying to save your life."

Her voice softened. "No, you don't have to."

"What happened at the ER? What did they do?"

"Nothing. They just let me sleep it off."

"How did you get home?" Ray suppressed a sob. "Joel told me you were just in your little nightie."

"They gave me three big flannel blankets and put me in a cab. They said I should keep the blankets."

Ray started to cry—God, how had he ever thought he did not love his wife? What had he done to her, and them? He had so fucked up his life!

His voice was wobbly. "Why did you OD? Were you trying to kill yourself?"

"No, not at all. I think I only took two of each. I was just trying to feel better. But my judgment was pretty impaired by then."

He wiped tears off his face with his bare hand, salt stinging the skin. "And how did you hit your head, do you know? You do tend to check out after you take your pills at night, even when it's only one."

"I know. It's really embarrassing. I have no idea how I did it or why I was in the hall in my nightgown. I might have gone down to get something from the laundry room, but why I didn't wear a robe, I'll never know. Or maybe I was trying to ask Joel for help, because I knew I'd taken too much, and I passed out on the way. I'll tell you one thing, I'm getting off of pills, all of them. Never again."

"And you taught today with a black eye?"

"Yes." She sounded almost amused. "I said my horse tripped and fell on his head, and when he surged back up, he smacked my cheek with his hard noggin. You remember, that did happen once, but my helmet protected me. Any rider would see right through that."

"So what did you tell them at the barn?"

"I told the truth. Those are my buddies there."

He could just imagine what that crew of harpies, her trainer and the other women riders, thought of him.

But as for Abby, he felt longing shoot through him, to be where she was, put ice on her cheek. It was the only thing that could make him feel all right.

Abby's voice sounded hard now, stern. "I really think you should go be with her. I've had enough of this. Go to Montreal."

Panic made him shake—he didn't even want that now.

"Oh, Bean," he whispered. "Don't give up on us. We'll get through this. It's just a crazy year, with the job and everything. I love you. You know I love you. I'm going to get over her, I swear."

"Did you send that text to her, after I talked to you?"

"No." It hadn't even occurred to him. In fact, he hadn't actually sent anything to Tory since he left Montreal. "I've broken it off with her. Don't you realize that? It's over with. It's you I love. Isn't it obvious? I've been frantic all day. You're my wife. It's very hard, but it's finished with her."

She didn't speak for half a minute, and when she did, she sounded disgusted. "Well, if that's true, you should tell her so, but don't declare your eternal love for her at the same time. You can't have it both ways. You should tell her you love me, if that's why you're doing it."

Ray felt a rush of, what—anger? Or guilt? She shouldn't tell him what to do. Yet she was right. For once he tried to let it blow through him and dissipate. "I know. I just wanted to give her something on my way out. I feel like I've toyed with her. And that's when a man's most likely to say stupid stuff like that, over-the-top stuff. It doesn't really mean anything."

Abby was quiet for a while, not contradicting him. "Well, if it is over with her, we'll have to see what you and I can manage. I really have had enough of this. I'm not going to take much more."

Chastened, he said, "I know you have, sweetheart, and I'll make it up to you. Just give me a little time."


HE DIDN'T WRITE to Tory—he put it off from one day to the next. Instinct said even to touch her name in the message app would be to play with fire. He spent as much time as he could with his favorite grad students and packed boxes to ship to Berkeley and Florida.

Because he was leaving, his students organized an evening tribute for him, with testimonials and readings from his work. Johnny flew in for it, and several other poets drove there or took the train, Walt coming from Harvard, his old friends Pete up from Maryland and Ellen from Pittsburgh, where they used to teach together.

The event was in a big elegant room, and it was packed, with about five hundred people listening, some students sitting on the floor. One by one his friends stood at the microphone, took turns telling stories about him and reading their favorites of his poems. All of his colleagues showed up, too, except for the Mouth Breather and Gumby.

When Hank went up there, his eyes became shiny, and he seemed genuinely heartbroken to see Ray go. When they finally led him to the microphone, Ray had to struggle to hold back tears himself.

This time Abby had not even seemed to consider flying in, and that made him sad—it was like he was on probation now. At the grad student party afterward, he gave her a call, so she would not wait up for him. She sounded cautious, and when they signed off, he felt sudden urgency.

"I love you," he said. "You know that, right? I love you." This time, he did cry.

Late that night, when the party broke up and everyone else went off to find some place to sleep, he ended up with Ellen in an all-night diner downtown, waiting for biscuits and gravy to show up. Ellen was an old salt from a fishing village up in Maine, and the only person he knew who still smoked cigarettes. She was also a decent poet and good friend. He could always count on her to hit him with the truth.

He had put away a vat of beer at the party, and in a sudden fit of alcoholic weepiness, he told her the whole sordid story, about Tory and Abby and himself.

Ellen laughed and lit a smoke. Dragging on it, she exhaled above his head. "Christ, Abby is a saint. I would have sliced your dick off a long time ago."

# TEN

ABBY SWORE OFF Ambien and Xanax, after that night in the ER. She iced her cheek and told herself she could leave Ray, just to see how that would feel. But did she want to be alone in her sixties? It was like looking down a long, empty corridor. The thought of all that echoing loneliness was frightening.

Ray sent her his new manuscript, *Star Viscera*, filled with poems he had been working on for years. The first warm week, she took it to a bench in the backyard and read it, corrected his spelling, and made notes on the lines that worked and the ones that needed another try. The poems made her ache, they were so good, even when she laughed—it was clearly going to be his best book yet. Working on it gave her a sense of purpose, a mission. She had always done that for him, since his first book, tried to make him the best poet he could be. Sometimes she had even given him titles and images, a line here and there, and she wasn't ready to relinquish that. She wanted to be part of it.

The truth was, there was glamor in the poetry world, and she didn't count much on her own, with one puny book, especially not since the Joyce study came out. People liked to slot you into one genre, and when she defected to literary criticism, it was as if the Joyce book ate the one of poems. Most of Ray's were dedicated to her, and almost no one knew about the crack in their façade, as a literary power couple still. She wanted to fly wherever he read from the new book and bask in the glow of his fame, be at the parties afterward with friends. She wasn't giving up their poet friends! Not Johnny, Ellen, Walt and Clarice, Hank and Priscilla, or any of the rest, all of whom she liked, no sir.

After she sent Ray her notes, she felt a strong new urge to write more poems. Mornings when she didn't have to teach, she walked down to his café, ordered lattes like he did, though his were decaf, cardiologist's orders—"unleaded," she and Ray called that, and hers had lead.

She wasn't going to write anymore about the marriage—she would write about things she thought or saw. She found a poem she wrote in grad school days, when she lived alone in a first-floor studio. At Ray's favorite table, up on the promontory over the front door, she did another draft of it with her Montblanc.

RATTLESNAKE

You would not have thought I could change
my stride in time, running so hard past the dark
glen where anyone could hide that I was off
the ground, in low earth orbit, when I saw my ankle
inches from its head, shoe about to mash
its tail. But eye to brain to spine to thigh, a million
quick cells cocked to fire, arching my leg an inch
to miss the snake.

New-hatched blackjack body, rusty diamonds
gleamed, three milk-white rattles fresh as baby
knuckles. It did not move, and wondering if it
was alive, I leaned my face closer. Blithe scales
prickled, changing shape. I froze, a reflex.

I was not afraid of it, not enough afraid, I think,
though I am afraid of many things, like Stinky,
the famous rapist on my street, who hides in single
women's houses till they fall asleep, his smell
of gasoline and sweat. Or the bull-size man
who not quite killed a woman running on this trail.
Afraid of atom bomb, cattle prod, retrovirus, legs
cut off in car crash, rain-soaked mudslide pouring
in my windows in the night.

But I was not afraid of this snake.
I crouched there till my legs went numb,
its round, flat, black eyes watching me.
I could have looked at it forever, held it,
let it bite me, swallowed it, worn it around
my neck like a lavaliere—but that wouldn't
be enough. What I wanted was to be it
or another like it, next to it in the warm dirt,
be it and still see it, its lover, a killer and so fine.

One of Ray's manual typewriters sat on his desk, and when she
walked home, she used it to type another draft. It was tough on the
fingers, but it felt more authentic to hammer for it, rather than to
glide with the computer's grace. *Clack clack clack*, she filled the air

with sound like Ray did, though she wasn't blasting music at the same time, a change the neighbors must have liked. Once when he was there, a woman from downstairs came up to say her teenage daughter couldn't stand the music anymore.

"And she's a teenager!" she had exclaimed.

RAY CAME HOME for the whole summer, and after a while he had declared his love for her enough that she started to relax. Though she watched for signs of change, he still lit up at the sight of her, if they hadn't met for a few hours.

But he was pale and thin, his face gray if he had to walk back up the hill, and most days she picked him up outside the gym. With his shirt off, she could see the beating of his too-big heart, under his left pec.

They went to see Dr. Death, and as usual Abby sat in the examining room and took notes. The doctor said Ray was doing much better than expected—though he also mentioned that it might be time to put him on the transplant list.

Ray left his office in a rage. "They have no idea what's wrong with me. I'm supposed to be a cripple now, and I'm just not. I can still swim half a mile. Okay, I have to stop at the end of every lap, but that still makes me superman, if my heart's as wrecked as they say. They can't explain it, and I'm not letting them cut my chest open. Indigestion. That jerk thinks my chest pain is indigestion!"

Abby looked at him anxiously. "But the guy in Providence admitted it might be your heart."

"Yeah. They don't even agree with each other. Until they do, they can just keep those big knives to themselves."

The house in Providence sold, and they planned the move. U of Miami had found them a house to rent, home of a math professor who would be away, and Abby would be on sabbatical that fall, so she could go along and look for a place to buy.

She would also visit local barns and have Beau shipped if she found one she liked—though Ray was getting vocally opposed again, complaining about her "hobby" and how much she spent on it. He had given several readings that spring, and when the paychecks arrived for them, she had deposited them in their joint account, out of which she paid for all of their Berkeley expenses, including Beau's stall and training fees, but also their mortgage, condo dues, property taxes, insurance, utilities, and food. But Ray seemed to think that money should be handed to him, though he was living there.

"You stole my Stanford check!" he shouted at her one night.

She looked at him cross-eyed. "Stole it how? It went into our joint account."

Had living apart so much that year made him think their finances were separate? But they weren't—they had been pooled for a quarter century, during which Abby had usually made more than he did.

And she couldn't take him seriously when he objected to the horse, in part because half the time he was generous about it, telling her to go to a horse show and have some fun—though A-class shows like the ones her trainer went to cost thousands of dollars for less than a week.

"Why don't you go to Pebble Beach?" he said enthusiastically one night. "It's your vacation. We can stay in Carmel again."

They had done it a few summers in a row, and though Ray was quickly bored with the show itself, he liked running on the white sand beach, eating in the restaurants, and browsing little shops on

Ocean Avenue. In one of them he had almost bought a nearly fifty-thousand-dollar Dürer woodcut, a brush with extravagance that gave the lie to his equine objections now.

IN JUNE, THE day before their anniversary, Abby went to the Bone Room to buy a gift for him. Ray loved bugs, and the shop had a collection of framed moths and beetles, as well as intact skeletons of bats and lizards. An enormous, live blond python lay draped along a shelf, flesh as dense as gold bullion, its eye on the patrons. From time to time its yellow tongue flickered out.

She picked out a giant pale green moth with slender tails at the bottom of each wing like a medieval lady's trailing sleeves and had them wrap it in the black skull-and-bones paper she knew would gladden Ray's heart.

She shopped for a card and bought one with a tiny white silk wedding gown on a real wire hanger pasted on the front. Inside of it she wrote, "Happy twenty-fifth to the love of my life." For too long, she had not said that to him, out of resistance to his craziness. But maybe it was time to say it now.

Next morning, they made love, wistfully, aware of all they had been through.

Afterward she handed him the skull-and-bones package. He clutched it, blue eyes bright. "Not till we get something for you. Let's go to the city."

The day was fine, sunny and warm. They put the top down on the Porsche and drove across the bridge to San Francisco, parked near Washington Square, and had brunch at Mama's: crab benedicts, strawberries with whipped cream, and champagne. They prowled through North Beach and Chinatown, looked at hand-painted Florentine crockery, dollhouse miniatures, and embroidered linens.

"Hey," Ray cried, inspired. "You need a new pen!"

The Montblanc she had loved for decades, Ray's first present to her, had lately fallen from her car at the barn and been crushed by a passing tractor. Since then Ray had made more than the usual remarks about barns, horses, and tractors, but now he seemed to light up and glow. He led her to the Montblanc store near Union Square and picked out a silver pen, though the price tag said nine hundred and fifty bucks. Over a thousand with taxes.

"It's perfect for our silver anniversary," Ray said, holding it out to her.

"Actually, it's platinum," the saleswoman said. "And it's refillable. No cartridges required."

It was lovely, gleaming, and it fit perfectly in Abby's hand.

"We'll engrave it for free," the woman said.

Abby wanted it to be her married name, Abigail McCormick-Stark. She wrote it out on the pad for testing pens.

Ray's face went a shade more pale. "What? No. You've never used it."

In fact, they had both used it that first heady year and called themselves the McCormick-Starks. But he seemed to have forgotten that.

The saleswoman looked at it on the pad. "It's too many letters, I'm afraid."

"All right," Abby said. "Just my first initial then. A. McCormick-Stark."

Ray's face was mulish. "You can't use that."

Abby refused to absorb what he had said.

The saleswoman stared at them. "We may just be able to fit that in." She scuttled toward the workshop in back.

\* \* \*

FOR THE NEXT month, when Ray walked down to his café, Abby used the beautiful new pen to write a poem. One morning he went out for a run first thing, leaving his phone behind, and on impulse she checked his texts, no password required.

"I'm so glad you're out getting fresh air," Tory had written just after he left.

He had sent her three messages while Abby was asleep, nothing of significance, remarks about the weather and a joke he'd heard— no plans to elope, not even any fond remarks. It meant nothing, surely, when Abby was there, moving to Miami, sleeping beside him every night. It was a habit, checking texts and sending them all day, just chatter, and of course he was concerned for Tory. She had been his student, and he felt guilty. He wanted to make sure she'd be all right.

As the time before they were to leave began to shrink, they invited friends over, Sateesh and Gloria, other local poets, and a few of Abby's colleagues. They took hikes along the coast, and spent an afternoon at the San Francisco Zoo. In the aviary, they held cups of nectar as lorikeets landed all over them. The tiny bright parrots enraptured Ray, who let them peck his buttons, pull his hair, a look of childlike wonder on his face. They spent an hour in the new giraffe house, with its extremely tall and narrow doors. Abby had once dreamed that a herd of giraffes had chosen her as their human, and it was a luminous dream, one of her best ever. Today at the zoo two babies had just been born, wobbly miniatures of their moms, who licked their coats with long blue tongues.

Next morning the front page of the *San Francisco Chronicle* ran a photo of one mother giraffe, who had dropped dead, hours after they watched her.

Abby started to cry. "How could that happen?"

A peculiar look crossed Ray's face. "That neck's a bitch to pump blood up, and she just gave birth. Heart strain."

Abby pressed a hand to the left side of his narrow chest, where it was shuddering. "How do you feel?"

He shrugged. "The usual. Midline pain. Not worth a shit."

"We've got to get someone to listen about that. Maybe your Miami cardiologist will have a better idea."

He looked away. "They're all the same. They can't do anything for me."

"Well, next summer, we at least need to get you a car for here," Abby said. "Or a scooter if you'd rather, so you don't need to walk up the hill."

She had tried before to get him Berkeley wheels, and once they had gone to look at Vespas in Oakland, all of them in cute pastel colors. But Ray had said he didn't want to have another big thing to take care of, with two houses and two cars already.

Now he said only, "We'll see."

He flew to Providence to finish boxing up his things and meet the moving van.

The night before he left, they made love in the dark at bedtime, though these days they rarely did it then. But she knew he liked the idea of doing it at night, and after his plane left, she texted him. "We should do it at night more often."

As soon as he landed, he wrote back, "Don't get used to that."

But he must have meant he was usually too tired then.

Three days later, she got a text from him about his scorn for all things Brown, written as he sat on a plane in Providence, waiting to fly back. How thank God he'd never have to be polite to those bastards again, and what a crook their realtor was, and how he was going to cut off her head. He didn't trust the movers, either. "They'll probably just lose our stuff. And I'll never speak to Hank again."

"Oh, sweetie," she wrote back. "Of course you will. You love Hank."

"Oh, I know," he wrote. "I know it'll be all right. I'll just keep smiling my Tory smile, and everything will be just fine."

Abby screamed and dropped the phone onto the couch, but it rang.

"I'm so sorry. I'm a jerk," he said. "That wasn't meant for you."

"No kidding. Were the others for her, too?"

"No, I was writing both of you. But my fingers are too big. They hit the wrong message and I write back too fast. I had to let her know what's going down."

Abby bit her tongue. I'll just keep smiling my Tory smile?


BY THE TIME she met him at the airport, she was determined not to mention it.

But she was tense and suspicious, and when he went out to try to run, she unpacked his suitcase, looked for evidence. Had the girl met him in Providence? She could just see them strolling on Conimicut Point Beach, holding hands, and agonized, trying to decide if they could part for good. But she found no clues.

A few days later, it was his fifty-third birthday, and Abby gave him an iPod, so he could easily take his music collection to Florida.

That night she was in bed trying to sleep, which was still hard without the drugs. And Ray had a light on a few feet away, using her laptop to transfer CDs to the iPod.

"Come to bed, sweetie, it's late," she said.

He kept his eyes on the screen and let his fingers rattle the keyboard.

She tried again. "Hey, sweetie, it's midnight. Please come to bed."

His voice was calm. "I will divorce you. I'll go live somewhere else."

Abby sat up, quivering. "What?"

He didn't answer, and she got out of bed in her nightgown. Crouching beside him, she tried to get into his line of sight.

"You just said you would divorce me! Do you even realize that?"

He refused to look at her, eyes unwavering on the screen.

"I will divorce you," he repeated like a machine. "I'll go live somewhere else."

"Ray! You just said you would divorce me and go live somewhere else!"

Still he did not look at her. In a monotone, he said, "I did not."

"Yes, you did. You said it twice!"

"I did not."

"What's going on? You said you would divorce me twice. You said it like a robot."

Eyes on the screen, he said, "I did not. You're insane. I'll have you committed for saying that. You won't remember any of this in the morning. Why don't you just pass out? It can't be long now. I'm sick of your walkabouts. Now shut up or I really will. I'll have you committed."

Abby crawled back into bed. Had she blacked out so many times he now assumed she would do it every night? Had he said things like that before and she had no memory of it? Well, now her mind was clear. She had heard every word.

When he finally turned the computer off, he did not come to bed. She heard him get a beer and pop it open. His phone went *ping* as it received a text.

In the morning, he brought her tea in bed as if nothing was wrong. She looked at him. "Do you remember what you said last night?"

His face went neutral. "What did I say?"

She told him. "You said it like a zombie, and then you denied saying it. You wouldn't even look at me. It was extremely scary. Were you trying to drive me nuts?"

He shrugged. "I'm surprised you remember it. Usually you don't."

"Of course I remember it. I told you, I went off the pills. You're the one who acted like you'd been body-snatched." Involuntarily, her voice shot to a higher register, throat tense. "Do you mean you've said stuff like that to me before?"

"If I did, you wouldn't remember it. I'm sorry. I've had a lot on my mind."

"Like what, the move? Your heart?" She had to force herself. "Tory?"

He had his daypack on, ready to walk to the café. "I don't want to talk about it."

"Are you still in contact with her?"

"You have to give me time. She was important to me."

Abby clung to that past tense.

He bent to give her a quick kiss. "Have a good morning."

She was afraid and mortified for both of them. What drove a man to torture his wife when he thought she would not remember it? It must be rage, at Brown, at the friends he thought were failing him, at himself for his stupid crush, and at her for not doing exactly as he wished, as if she were one of his arms. Maybe most of all, at his heart for what was happening to it, enraged and afraid. He was helpless against most of that, and there she was, six feet away, supposedly unconscious, like a fly he could pull the wings off of for fun.

Outside, it looked like rain, though it never rained in August in Berkeley. She had promised the other condo owners she would dispose of the old paint people had left in the basement. They shared chores, and that was her summer assignment.

But first, she got out her platinum pen. In this poem it would be February, the way it looked, and the lunatic she lived with would be Berryman's tender, sad Henry, whom she had always liked.

### MY LIFE AS A GOAT

It's gray and windy out, on the verge of rain
and I can barely lift my arms because of the triceps
dips I started with a sadistic trainer, or maybe sadistic
trainer is redundant. "You can't leave him alone like
this," his friend said. "We count on you to keep him
calm. You're the goat in the stall with the race horse."
Have you ever noticed "die" inside of "diet"? "Other"
in "mother"? I wanted to mother an other, but my other
wanted me to mother him, and now he wants another
other. So let's take the toxic waste to the dump and stand
in a puddle while we pour it out. You once said it was fun
to go to the gas station with me. Does that apply
to the hazmat site? And is that why you were so mean
to me last night? Chafing at the beloved because,
well, she's there, and the ones you want to lash
or lay are not. Oh, Henry, come smell
the Japanese mock orange trees as they riot
outside in the February night, sweeter than lilac,
more poignant than rose, like you and me and our long life.

She thought of Ray's face beaming as she walked toward him, when he met her in airports. When they got married, they had decided to do it privately, no families, just Johnny and one other friend as witnesses, in the Morgantown courthouse. She had worn a tan skirt suit and a pale sunhat and flats, Ray in an ancient gray wool jacket and slacks, Johnny as best man in a green polo shirt with a hole in one sleeve. But Johnny had brought a bouquet for her, and when they left the courthouse and stepped onto the street, people rushed out of stores to ask, "Did you just get married?"

They had made lunch for the friends, and a few hours later, alone again, she and Ray had walked to the little bookstore downtown through the summer evening light. On the way they spied a pair of redheaded woodpeckers high up in a dead tree.

You could mark off the stages of their life with birds: the baby jays, the rose-breasted grosbeaks in their West Virginia yard, which also showed up at their feeder in California, far out of range, seeming to follow them cross-country, like a cat walking to reclaim its former home. White pelicans and white-tailed kites out near Point Reyes, tiny screech owls in Providence.

In Florida, there might be pink flamingos and scarlet ibises. Roseate spoonbills. Swallowtail hummingbirds blown north by hurricanes. But she had not bought a Florida bird book, and now she supposed she never would.

# ELEVEN

IT WAS A COLD, foggy August morning in Berkeley, the kind Ray loved, as he sat in his café and tried to write.

They were leaving in four days, and he tried to imagine a journey he could take to paradise, and what it would be like. Not an actual place like Miami, or even the more crazy-named Florida towns, like Two Egg, Sopchoppy, Ocheesee, and Yeehaw Junction—but a utopia with infinite record stores, all free, and Salvador Dalí taking his anteater for a ride on the Metro. Where the cheesesteaks had no calories, and you aged backward after forty, till you got to twenty, then forward again, keeping what you knew and getting smarter all the time, and richer and handsomer. Where you could go to any time in history, converse with Keats or Rimbaud or Duchamp, and come right back. Where funny-looking guys like him were the most desirable, and girls wore bikinis all year round, because it was never cold. Not that he could take that now, when his heart felt swollen as a baked apple, ready to split open wide.

He scratched all that onto a yellow pad, jumped up and strode out to the Ave, down to Moe's and Amoeba. There would be book and record stores in Miami, but probably in strip malls, the stock all new and suitable for Christian youth. Nothing like the raunchy blast of Amoeba, with its barrio mural on an outside wall, its bins of mostly used CDs, and some vinyl, recycled by guys with kaleidoscopic taste. He could just imagine who they were, hanging out in garrets since the sixties, gray beards yellow from dope smoke, able to discourse on Nietzsche or John Cage or Mario Savio, who of course they knew, along with Julia Vinograd, who sold her poems one at a time to patrons in cafés. There might be one or two such characters in Florida, but inflected with an awful Southern twang, living in swamps and wrestling alligators, unaware of the twelve-tone scale or the major figures of Japanese jazz—toothless guys who played banjo and harmonica and knew where to find great black blues singers in remote shacks.

There had never been a place that fit him the way Berkeley did, though Providence sometimes came close. And now Providence was off-limits forever. He would never visit there. Instead he was about to go live in a house he'd never seen, in a town he could barely picture, having been there only once. And while he had not snapped the string that connected him to Berkeley, it had never felt so tenuous.

To distract himself, he bought every disk that caught his eye, stuffed them in his pack, walked to the Cal gym and lifted weights, showered and dressed again. He was having a farewell lunch with Sateesh, and he sent a quick message to Tory first.

"Off to lunch with Sateesh. Saying good-bye to this place is sad."

"Yeah, moving is hell," she wrote back. "But at least you'll be on the correct coast then."

She added a smiley face wearing sunglasses. She had started sending emojis, and it made him feel like a pedophile. How young exactly was that girl?

Sateesh picked him up outside the gym, looking the opposite of a Berkeley resident, in a shiny black Lincoln Town Car, like someone from the diplomatic corps, Sateesh in the driver's seat smoking a cigar. He had on a fedora, for Christ's sake, and a tweed overcoat. But Sateesh had read everything, and if you wanted to talk to someone about Rimbaud, or Simon Schama on the French Revolution, Sateesh was your man.

They went as usual to Brennan's, down near the highway, the least pretentious of old Berkeley dives, where you could get turkey and mashed potatoes with gravy any day of the year and wash it down with a selection of draft beers.

They sat in a corner booth, out of everyone's earshot, and as usual Sateesh spoke in a low, conspiratorial voice. "So how's your home life?"

Ray felt his chest constrict. "I'm being horrible. Sometimes I think the only way to stop it is to leave."

Sateesh shook his head. "You're too hard on yourself, man. I still don't understand why you stayed with her after that affair. If Gloria had the nerve to run around on me, she would be toast. And of course I'd kill the jerk, whoever he was. I still think you should let me do something to that Jacob fellow."

Sateesh claimed to be related to some Mumbaikar mobsters, and he had seriously offered to have Jacob "taken out" after that semester in New York.

But while Ray often gave vent to feelings of that kind, that's all it was. He sometimes had to express his wrath at some object, but he had never thrown a punch in his life. And seriously, have someone killed? Naaaaah. He was clear on that. It cheered him up to realize it. Maybe he was not such a bad guy.

"Hey, man, look," he said now, running both hands through his hair. "I'm not positive she had an affair. It looked fishy as hell, but never mind. It's ancient history now. I've got other stuff to think about, like moving to fucking Florida. *That* feels like going over the falls backward. I mean, where the hell is Miami? I'm so sick of moving around."

"But you'll be back next summer?" Sateesh said. "Maybe Christmas, too? You're not renting out the apartment here, correct?"

He shook his head. He and Abby hadn't even talked about doing that, with things so uncertain between them. Some days he felt the way he did in restaurants, when he couldn't decide what to order. At their favorite bistro, he could never choose between the steak frites and the crab-stuffed sole, and he wouldn't know which one he was going to tell the waiter till he heard the words come from his mouth. He wasn't sure which way he was going to jump. Take Abby to Florida, or go alone and see Tory? Tory, whom he didn't know at all. He'd had lunch with her a few times, but he'd never seen her naked or slept next to her. They chatted electronically all day, but really what could you tell from that? She didn't know him, either. It was like one long phone call before a first date.

"I'll tell you one thing," Ray said slowly. "I think Abby left this marriage a long time ago. It's been years now since she really noticed me. She doesn't realize that I'm half dead. The only time she pays attention to me is when we have a fight, and I think that's having a bad effect on my health."

Sateesh was alarmed and wanted all the details, what his doctor was saying now. "Listen. If you need to leave Abby, Gloria and I will support you all the way. Whatever you have to do. If you want to come move in with us tonight, you can. We hate houseguests, but we'd do anything for you."

Ray nodded and fought the urge to cry. "I know you would. Thank you, man, I appreciate it. But if you want to know the truth, I don't know what I'm going to do. I've never been able to picture the future. It seems to me like a laughable concept, when we all could die tonight. I certainly could. And one thing is for sure, whatever happens next will be different from whatever you thought it would be. So I mostly try not to imagine it."

THAT AFTERNOON THE sky cleared, and Ray and Abby went to Monterey Market to shop. After her run, they made chicken piccata and he put it in the oven for the final bake, while she got in the tub.

Ray opened a bottle of sauvignon blanc and took it in the bathroom with two stem glasses, poured while he perched on a tall stool by the bath and handed one to her. The room had six-foot-tall French windows facing west, and when the sun sank over the coastal mountains, the light went gold, then pink, shading to blue. Ray held his glass up to the last pink rays to make it blush. He felt a rush of well-being.

"Damn, Bean! I think it's all finally happening for me. I think this job is going to do it. I'm finally getting what I deserve, a real endowed chair and some respect. I even think my heart is going to do better there, now that all that shit with Brown is done. Fuck them completely, even Hank. Things will never be the same with him. There's a bitterness there now. He did nothing to get me the job, and you know he could have. He could have made it happen. His silence, that was the death knell. But damn, I'm going to be the Dudley Harrington Chair of Poetry at Miami. Fuck Brown!"

He went in his study next door and put on one of his new CDs. He had listened to them all that afternoon, and one of the Ryuichi Sakamoto was fine.

"Here, listen," he called to her. "There's a killer riff in this."

A clarinet slashed through the air, attacked on the slant by a trombone. In the study, he opened the tin where he kept roaches, took one out, lit his Bic, and pulled on it, just a tiny hit to keep the euphoria going.

Playing imaginary drums, he bopped back into the bathroom, where the air was filled with the smell of Abby's pricey white gardenia soap, while she lay long and languid in the tub, pale hair bunched up and tied on top of her head to keep it dry. She looked lovely, but self-absorbed as usual. She didn't say anything about the music.

Instead she tried to tell him about some kerfuffle in her department, a New Historicist man who wanted tenure, though he was opposed by the ruling theory coalition. Ray hated the people she worked with. The last time he made the mistake of going to a Cal party with her, people had treated him like someone's boring spouse. They called themselves literary professionals, and none of them read contemporary poetry.

He tossed back his wine. "Those jerks you work with are just ignorant. They're snobs and parasites with too much sense of entitlement."

She lifted her head and looked at him. "That's a bit of a generalization. Some of them are all right."

He felt the lift as the dope came on—he decided to let that pass, what she had said. "What about you? What's your next move? Any big plans for your sabbatical?"

She looked evasive. "I've started something, actually."

Ray nodded. "Great."

They both believed in keeping their work hush-hush till it was done, when they would show it to each other. So he didn't ask for more right then.

He went to the kitchen and made salad, rubbing the big wooden bowl with garlic, slicing the intriguing purple radishes they'd bought. He changed the record, played another killer riff, stopped off for another hit of dope. Cranked, he whirled around the kitchen, washing, chopping, throwing things into the bowl.

"Did you do dope?" Abby called over the music as she came into the kitchen, wearing a white *yukata* printed with blue flowers, its hem trailing on the floor, its flamboyant square sleeves balancing her height. Her fair hair was still piled on top of her head, and she left it there, showing off her long pale neck.

"Yeah, a little bit," he said, and grinned. "How can you tell?"

She snorted. "Because you always ask me what I want to be when I grow up, something like that."

He opened another bottle while he served dinner and kept their glasses filled. The piccata came out great, the salad a good balance of crisp and smooth, sweet and tart. He finished fast as usual, while Abby picked at it—she seemed to eat slower every year.

But he jumped up and kept the music coming, on the living room system now. The DVD player was on the table, hooked to the screen, and he slid in the latest from Netflix and pushed "Play."

Abby tried to get between him and the screen. "Hey, if you're going to watch a movie, could you turn the music off?"

Instantly, unreasonably annoyed, he tried to ignore her. For five minutes, he didn't move, and finally she got up and switched the music off.

Why did she have to be such a killjoy anyway? She was always worried about the neighbors and what they thought. Why couldn't she let him have his innocent pleasures? He let her have hers, and hers weren't innocent. She'd spent how many thousands on that horse? And on a Porsche that gobbled up over a thousand bucks every time she took it to the shop. She drove the thing to the barn and left him stranded here without even a way to go to the grocery store. She stole his Stanford check!

Calmly, keeping breathing, eyes on the screen, he thought it through. He was going to be the goddamn Harrington Chair of Poetry, and it was time he got some respect, at home as well as in the world. They would live by his rules. Starting with the horse.

Not looking at her, he said, "Things are going to have to change. We're not taking that horse to Florida. We can't afford it. You should sell the thing. Every cent I make, you blow on that horse, or your fucking car. I'm sick of it."

With a clank, Abby put down her fork. "We've been over this. I spend my own money on riding. I'll do that this fall, too."

"Oh, yeah? Well, what did you do with my Stanford check, and the one from McGill? I never saw either one of them, and you've spent them already. Where's the damn checkbook?"

"Where it always is, in my desk."

"Yeah, in your desk. You think the money is all yours." He went to get it.

When he came back, her face was red. Hotly, she said, "Do you live in the eternal now? I supported you for about ten years."

He laughed, as he flipped the check register. "You always say that, and it isn't fucking true. I supported myself just fine before we met. You think you can live like a rich person. You have a rich person's hobby. Jesus, look at this!"

There was his check from McGill, fifteen hundred bucks, deposited, followed by checks she wrote, eight hundred to her trainer, six hundred to the barn, and who the fuck was Pete McLaughlin and why did she give him one-fifty?

"My McGill check, and poof, you spent it all!"

Abby stood up, looking agitated now. "That's your account, too. You live here, remember? We have expenses here, and you get the benefit of all of it, including the car. And do you really think I could have made it through the last few months without my horse, while you're off sending love notes to your girlfriend all day long? You do realize, don't you, it's illegal to do that with one of your students?"

What a pathetic move that was, so low. "She's not my student anymore. Don't change the subject. I'm sick of how you take my money without even asking me. That has to stop right now."

Abby looked wild, like she was starting to lose it. "You live here, too. That's a joint account. What, am I supposed to pay for everything and you can be a houseguest and spend all your money on CDs?"

Hah! That dead issue again. "Will you ever shut up about that? A CD is nothing compared to what you're doing, sitting in the saddle ripping up hundred-dollar bills."

She seemed to make a huge effort to calm her voice, as if that would mean she'd won the argument. "But they're my hundred-dollar bills. You've never made as much as me. This coming year is the first time you will ever make more than I do."

Something exploded in his chest—he flung the checkbook past her, and it hit a wall. "Shut up about that! It's not true. I've made more than you for years. People pay thousands to hear me read, and my books fucking sell. I make royalties."

Her face was pinched with the effort to seem calm. She stood three feet away from him, not moving. "You want to see the tax records? Half-time teaching is half pay. Your gigs don't make up for that."

He stood up, retrieved the check record, and ripped it up. "You're always fucking undermining me. You wonder why I talk to that girl? I'll tell you why. She admires me. She thinks I'm wonderful. And you? What does my wife think? My wife steals my money, tells me I'm dirt. I'm sick of it. You sell that horse!"


HE SLEPT MAYBE an hour that whole night in the guest bed. The pain in his chest was crushing him, but that was nothing to the pain inside his head. He was a monster, or there was something monstrous inside of him. Sure, maybe it was Abby's fault. But now that was him, the monster husband, the monsband. The guy who tore up the check record and couldn't stand the truth.

Yeah, he hadn't made much in the early years. He was a grad student, then a Poet in the Schools. The first year they were married, he thought he was going to make eleven thousand dollars, and it turned out to be six, while Abby brought home twenty-five. The job in Pittsburgh had started five years in, and no, it didn't pay as much as she made by then.

He knew all that, and it was not a nice day when he realized it. But back then she admired him, loved his work, and she was tactful about their finances.

But couldn't she see that it tortured him? It made him feel helpless. His dead father hovered over him asking how he could let his wife make more. But not support him, no, she was wrong there—he could have lived on what he made.

And it broke his heart—was that what his chest pain was, a breaking heart?—the way she resented him. At first, they had been so tender together. He had a picture he had taken of her back then, holding a baby bunny she found in their yard in Morgantown, half the size of her palm, its eyes still closed, but trying to hop right there on her hand. It was on his desk—he turned on the light and looked at it. It made him want to cry—it was taken before the lupus, her hair a full blond cloud, her skin unlined and young, her perfect, sexy, cupid's-bow mouth with no fine lines around the upper lip. He put it facedown and switched off the light.

He was all ash inside, gray as the air in the room, graphite or lead. There was nothing he wanted to do, not even sleep. Sleep took too much energy.

Finally the clock said six. He could get up.

He washed his face and dressed. He brushed his teeth. He stood in the kitchen and waited till he heard Abby stir in their bedroom.

He walked in and sat down on her side of the bed, hip touching hers. He had not made her tea.

She sat up and quickly said, "I'm sorry. I'm really sorry for whatever I said last night. I had too much to drink."

Nothing in him answered that. He felt cold as ash.

The words came from his mouth. "I don't want to be married anymore."

There, he'd said it, asked for the steak frites instead of the sole.

Her voice pleaded, "Sweetheart, I know that was awful last night. Please. You know this has been rough for me, the past, what, almost eight months, since you told me about the girl."

He looked at her, but he wasn't there. He was somewhere else. He did not call her Bean. "I'm sorry, Abby. I just don't want to be married anymore. We don't have to rush into getting a divorce, and I promise you will not have to give up anything. You can keep riding. I'll make sure of it. But I've had enough."

He got up, walked to the kitchen, and stood there while she dressed.

She came in, pulling a small suitcase. "I'll go somewhere until you leave, so you can pack your things." She opened the back door and stopped, looking at him, her face pale under the riding tan. "I think you've lost your mind."

He nodded. "Yes, probably."

But now there was nothing he could do. He was just ash.

WITH THREE DAYS until he was to fly to Florida, he felt too sick to do anything, the pain in his chest like a tightening vise, like he was on the rack.

And how the hell was he supposed to pack his stuff, when he didn't have a car? He couldn't even get boxes to start. He couldn't go buy food—not that he could eat. But of course she didn't think of that, wrapped up in her narcissistic hurt.

He lay on the bed and on the couch. His phone rang and he didn't answer it. He did not check for texts. He didn't want to talk to anyone or explain himself. He was in deepest mourning, crushed, giving up his life, his wife, the place he loved. Hell, it had all been taken away from him already, and he was just facing it. Every gift had a little tag on it that said, THIS TOO WILL BE TAKEN AWAY. But this was a big one, worst loss of his life.

Two days to go, he tried to pull himself together, put on shorts and a tattered singlet and went out for a run, just in the neighborhood. The trouble was, nothing was flat there, it was either up or down. Down, he could lope reasonably well, and he made it to campus and circled around.

But up was something else, almost impossible. Struggling toward home, he had to walk the steepest part. When he reached the relative plateau after the worst hill, he could barely drag his feet, hoping his heart would slow down.

He was a block away from their building, when suddenly he saw a small, familiar pale yellow car, a Porsche, top down, driving toward him, familiar fair hair blowing in the driver's seat. Her face in large dark glasses didn't turn his way—but of course she could see him, half dead, barely moving on the sidewalk.

But did she stop and ask if he wanted a ride home? No—she did not slow down. She merely flicked one hand above the wheel and zoomed off down the hill.

# TWELVE

ABBY FELT LIKE half her cells had been ripped out in one quick jerk, leaving an outline but no real substance. She would not throw a shadow in sunlight. For three long nights, she lay on her trainer's couch, wept through the days.

A lawyer at the barn was adamant that she file for divorce at once.

"Divorce is about property, and you don't want to get screwed," she said.

She gave her three names, and it was something Abby could do, a project, between her and the abyss. She interviewed the two women lawyers first, on the phone.

The one man on the list asked her to come to his swanky eighth-floor office in downtown Oakland. He was handsome and neatly put together, with short white hair, crisp suit and shirt, and large brown eyes. He seriously interviewed her, about their marriage and finances, while Abby cried quietly. When the man found out Ray was about to move to Florida, he grew alarmed.

"Listen, you don't have to retain me. But even if you don't, we should file the papers today. In Florida they tend to favor the good ol' boys, and you could lose your condo. You might even have to pay alimony, because you partially supported him."

Abby protested. "He's about to start making thirty thousand more than me."

"Doesn't matter. Courts try to keep the same arrangement in divorce that applied in the marriage."

Aghast, Abby retained him on the spot, impressed that he was the only one who had thought of that. When the papers were ready, he sent them to the courthouse by courier and advised Abby to find a friend who was willing to serve them on Ray that day. She quailed at the thought, but called Sateesh and Gloria on their home phone.

"We don't want to be involved in that," Sateesh said gruffly.

"No, we don't," Gloria agreed on the extension phone.

They said nothing else, and she soon hung up, embarrassed and ashamed. And yet it was Ray's idea not to be married anymore, not hers.

Who to call? Back in Morgantown, her hairdresser had asked Abby to serve papers on her husband, and the man had practically punched her. She didn't want to put any of her colleagues or barn friends through that, and Joel was out of town.

The man who lived downstairs was a sweet-natured playwright named Charles, who left lights burning in his place all night. He and his wife were the only post-adolescents in Berkeley who still smoked, which could make Abby's bedroom smell like the bars in Providence. Charles also drank heroically, and when he had houseguests, he might go on a three-day bender, laughing and clinking ice cubes on his deck all night. He had once offered Ray a drink at dawn, when they met in the hall.

But he dressed well, in clean pressed shirts and pants, though he worked at home, and he could be charming and helpful when it came to sandbagging their steep driveway in storms and rescuing lost fawns—the neighborhood being full of nearly domesticated deer, who could be seen munching people's gardens down to stumps.

She met Charles on the corner near their building. He had a mobile face that could scrunch up in a pained way like a chimp's, and he grimaced as she handed him the fat white envelope, three lawyers' names embossed in one corner. He was back in five minutes.

"Was he there?"

"Oh, yes. And not too happy to see what I brought." He waved his arms. "I said, 'Don't kill the messenger!'"

Charles signed an affidavit with the date and time, and Abby took it to the lawyer's office and turned it in.

Then she had literally nothing else to do, on the worst-timed sabbatical in history. The minutes until Ray left stretched endlessly, like tar, like taffy, each one an hour long.

Finally it was the day of his flight, and in trepidation she went home, to the quiet, empty apartment—though he appeared to have left most of his things.

On the kitchen counter was a hand-printed note, on yellow legal paper.

*Abby,*

*Well—so much for slowing things down, and having that drunk hand me the papers was especially classy. Of course now that it's turned over to lawyers it will become adversarial—that's what they do, and after thousands of dollars it'll just come down to the same division we would do on our own. We know whose stuff is whose.*

*Of course I couldn't take mine now. We'll be able to work that out later I hope. I left the moth because I didn't have the heart right now to take it and it looks good behind the orchid. And that jacket of mine you look so good in, it can be yours.*

*I think this is something you've wanted for a while. We ruined this marriage together, and you had a big hand in ruining me as a husband. You'll be fine even if you don't get to take me to the cleaners. I love you but all I'll be able to picture for a while is that backhanded ta-ta wave you gave me as you drove by.*

*Ray*

She walked into his study and collapsed on the wood floor, one arm around his chair leg, and sobbed. She just could not believe that he was gone, that he didn't care. He hadn't even asked her where she went. Over a quarter century, he had made her account for every minute, and now he wasn't even curious.

It was too much to take in, and she had nothing else to think about. She was adrift in outer space. She was not a self. She was the wriggling cut-off half of a live creature. Those early years of making love three times a day must have smelted down her personality, making it part of his. Decades like that with him, and then nothing. She had no reason not to sob all day, all night. If only she could teach, go to faculty meetings, even serve on the college budget committee, it might anchor her.

But now nothing was required of her beyond watering her plants. Even her horse was cared for by her trainer and the grooms.

She drove out to the barn and stood with her arms around Beau's neck, pressing his big heart to hers, while he tucked his long chin against her back, like he was embracing her. A horse's heart radiates for sixteen feet, someone had said—radiates what, she wasn't sure. But it was the only thing that stopped the stabbing in her chest.

"NO MORE THINKING of Ray," Clarice texted her, two days after he left. "Time to move on to other loves. He's going to marry Tory. They will have kids, Abby."

That threw Abby on the floor again. Have children with Tory, when he had refused with her? She texted Ray and told him what she said.

"No kids," Ray wrote back. "Clarice is a snake. She knows nothing about me, and you seem to know less all the time."

Abby had been friends with Clarice since before they met their husbands. But she did not write back to her.

It was too easy now to understand how a person went berserk. She imagined flying to Florida, buying a rifle, and staking out his house—say, from the roof of a garage across the street. But unlike Ray, she was good at picturing the future, and the inside of a Florida prison was nothing she wanted to see. They probably used the electric chair on wives who murdered good ol' boys. Besides, it was one of those acts you would instantly regret and not be able to take back. No wonder Dieter killed himself.

But what was she supposed to do? Day after day, and then week after week, there was nothing. She tried to write poems, but they came out lifeless, hollow with despair. Sometimes she made a plan, drove to a restaurant, and could not get out of the car. All her life she had been decisive, but now she could not follow through with anything. Some nights she slept for twelve hours, living instead in vivid dreams, always with Ray in them.

As word of their separation spread, people she had known for years seemed at a loss for how to act or what to say. They looked away, like you do from someone missing a limb or with a deformed face—perhaps out of fear, of what could happen to a person just like them. Sateesh and Gloria lived half a mile away, but she did not hear from them. She called Gloria, who did not pick up at home or on her cell, and though she left messages, Gloria did not call back.

Finally, a month later, Gloria called twice, both times when Abby was riding and couldn't hear the phone. (Did Gloria remember when her lessons were?)

The first message said, "Oh, I'm so sorry, I just got your message on the home machine. I never listen to those, because it's usually Sateesh's father, calling to say how much he hates the nursing home. He calls fifteen times a day."

The second message said, "Oh, hi, just got your message on my cell. I never listen to those, because only Sateesh uses that number, and I know I'm going to see him soon."

Neither time did she suggest they meet.

And it was not only Sateesh and Gloria—all the people she and Ray had seen as a couple in Berkeley either did not think of her anymore, or felt they had to choose between her and Ray, and they went with him. For years, they had gone to dinners and parties with a wide circle of friends, but now she saw no one at all, except the women at her barn. Weekend nights filled her with dread. It had felt a bit like that with Ray in Providence, and yet each night she could look forward to his call.

She tried to distance the issue, make it theoretical. Was it just some sort of deep, basic preference for men, in a world where they were masters of the universe? Where *king* and *queen*, *master* and *mistress* had such different second meanings, the sleazy underside of the female nouns suggesting the cultural distrust of women that had been around since Eve. Did that mean a man could mistreat his wife and have it make no difference to their friends?

After all, the nation went on being friends with Bill Clinton, after his multiple adulteries. But just think, if Hillary had been caught having sex with an intern in the White House—or even if Bill had claimed she was—would she have a snowflake's chance of ever being president? And if Bill left her and married Monica, would Hillary be invited anywhere?

ONE DAY HER phone rang, just its ordinary ring, "Bad to the Bone"—it was Johnny, asking how she was. She told him she was being shunned and asked him why.

"Uh, well, Ray blames you quite a bit. It's only natural. No one wants to be the bad guy," Johnny said. "And after all, you did have that affair."

Slowly, carefully, Abby explained: she did not have an affair. Ray just thought she did. "And in this country, we assume innocence until guilt is proved. Isn't it obvious he's trying to deflect his own guilt? He can't stand being in the wrong."

Ray was from a blame culture, as Johnny probably knew. His family argued over who did what to whom, and no one ever blamed themselves when bad things happened.

She doubted Johnny was convinced, his loyalty to Ray too deep—even if they sometimes fought, Johnny would take Ray's word over hers. That rumor felt like quicksand, impossible to fight. She was Ann Boleyn, one day the queen, the next convicted of adultery she did not commit, in a dungeon waiting for the sword, while her husband bedded ladies-in-waiting.

She heard it again a few days later from Ray's friend Pete, calling from Maryland. Pete was a good guy, with a droll wit, and he had always made it clear that he was as much Abby's friend as Ray's. He had been to Miami to give a reading. Tory was there, and he had talked to her at the party afterward.

"I'm quite surprised," Pete said. "She looks like a little French doll, but she doesn't act like one. She's kind of prickly. More like beef jerky than a pillow."

Abby tried to laugh, but it came out a whimper—Ray showing off his little trophy girl, who was somehow tough and salty and high protein? Abby felt like she'd gone down a zip line and smashed into a tree.

Pete went on. "Johnny said a year ago that Ray was running amok. I told him to snap out of it, that it wasn't worth wrecking his life. You guys were married a long time."

"A year ago?" Abby gasped. "Are you sure?"

A year ago, he hadn't told her, but he had told Johnny? And probably Hank, and they talked about it with Pete. But no one had told her, though she considered all those guys her friends. She felt like a child the grown-ups had been lying to. Yes, there's a Santa Claus. No, Ray didn't sleep with Tory while he was with you. But would a man leave his wife without test-driving the other woman—a man who had grown up in the sexual free-for-all of the 1970s?

Pete cleared his throat. "Abby? Are you there? How are you taking all of this?"

Abby snorted. "Well, I'm getting over the urge to buy a gun."

Pete gasped. "Wow. You're giving me some insight into how Susie must have felt about Charlotte."

Abby laughed half hysterically. Susie had been Pete's longtime wife, mother of his kids, Charlotte the much younger woman he was now with. "What, when you left her for a grad student, you thought she wouldn't mind?"

She felt the urge to tell Ray, who at least understood that much. It was a reflex, wanting to share everything with him.

Pete groaned. "I guess I wasn't thinking about her. A common male failing."

Abby mused, "What I know about you poets makes me think about our affinity with chimps. They have mates but screw around as much as they can get away with. It might just have to do with opportunity, I guess. If women threw themselves at used car salesmen all the time, the way they do with you guys, they would do it, too."

Pete demurred. "I wouldn't say all the time. And some of us resist those chimp-like urges."

"Thank God for that." Abby paused. "Pete, is he telling people I had an affair?"

He sounded troubled. "I always thought that was unworthy of him, saying that. But, yeah, he said it again a few days ago."


SHE TAPPED OUT a text to Ray but did not send it. She would write a letter instead. Once and for all, spell it out on paper, something he could keep, what had and had not occurred between her and Jacob. Yes, Jacob was an attractive guy, and they had flirted in the beginning. But didn't Ray flirt, too? It was harmless, and anyway, Jacob might be gay. He seriously dieted, and the first time she saw him, when he walked into her office with late gold sun beaming through her window onto his face, she had thought at once, *Oh, too bad he's gay.* It was just an instinct, but she thought she might be right, whether he knew it or not. It might explain why every woman he dated ran for the hills.

But he had been a good friend, especially after Gillian was killed. The whole department came together then, and they were especially kind to Abby, as Gill's friend. After that, Jacob had signed his emails to her with an *x* and sometimes even *love*. But that was the most torrid thing that had ever happened between them.

She wrote that out for Ray, went for a run, and shoved the letter in a mailbox up the hill. Then she took a long route up the steep Berkeley ridge. Running could always make her angry, and for months now she had lectured Tory as she ran, about stealing another woman's man. Now she wanted to rant at Ray, as she pounded uphill, loped along the ridge, then down another way.

Back home, she texted Ray. "It's great to hear from your friends that I was the last to know you were 'running amok,' as one of them said to me today."

He wrote back instantly. "Running amok? I sold a book, got this job, taught full-time, and was on the cover of *APR*. Who was the asshole who said that?"

"Johnny to Pete last fall."

"That's it for Johnny, I swear. I hate everyone. Leave me alone."

BUT EVEN AFTER that exchange, he texted Abby several times a day, as if the habit were hard to break. They knew better than to speak on the phone, but it was hard to become hysterical with your fingers. Some nights he wrote bitterly, about how little attention she had paid to him and how upset he was that she had filed for divorce.

In despair, especially after a few drinks, Abby bit back. "Do you really not care at all about me now? We were not junior-high-school steadies, we were husband and wife." Or, "Is it just a coincidence that you stuck around while it was to your economic advantage, then vanished the second it was not?"

Some nights they did not fight. Once he wrote, "I am so sorry I broke the most important thing in my life. I could not unbreak it. It was twenty-five years of my life, too, and I will be bereft of us forever. But I couldn't go on being a husband worth a damn. Maybe it's my fault but I was desperately unhappy. I have been going through hell for a long time and dragging you with me. I don't want you to suffer, you who I promised to protect and broke that promise because I couldn't even protect you from me."

That sounded too glib—this was a guy who rarely apologized for anything. Had someone told him that was the way to manage her? He sounded like he felt just great.

"Are you with Tory right now?" she wrote back.

"Yes, I have seen Tory and I'm seeing her again."

She imagined running into them together. What would she do? Spring at Tory like a puma and rip off her face.

Angrily she wrote, "So glad you're getting laid tonight. Instead of imagining her while you're with me. Instead of texting her while I'm asleep."

"Yes, I was talking to her. So many of the awful things you say are true and I have been living with them. Peace, please. I don't need updates about how horrible I am."

Was it because he was afraid of getting old? One night that summer they had been in North Beach sitting over cioppino. For some reason, her run that day had made her left knee hurt, and she popped ibuprofen with her wine.

"Boy, it's hard getting older," she had ventured to say.

Ray had visibly recoiled. "Why the hell do you want to talk about that?"

Now she wrote wistfully, "I'm sorry I'm getting old. You must have felt like death was getting into bed with you."

He replied at once. "You didn't make me feel like that, dummy. Chalk it up to my horrible character, but not that."

Some mornings she apologized. "There's a program that blocks you from sending email written late at night. Needed also for texts. I should not have said what I did."

"Beanie, let's make one thing clear. You never, ever have to apologize to me."

He let her know when he bought a house and when Tory moved down there to live with him. But even after that, he sometimes texted Abby half the night. He often seemed to be awake, though it was three hours later there. It could feel like old times, the two of them talking intimately in the night, as they always had.

"Just don't marry her the second we're divorced, okay?" she wrote. "That would be an insult to our marriage."

He didn't seem to notice what she'd said. Instead he answered, "Sometimes I miss having a life, being surrounded by people who cared for me even if it was an illusion. As illusions go, it was a good one. You I know are real."

"Yes, I am. I always loved you. But you have a life now, right, with Tory? Why aren't you answering my question? It's urgent to me."

"I won't marry her as soon as we get divorced. My new life, we will see, but yes, it's obviously, considering what I've done, worth a real shot."

So he was going to marry her. Abby did not write back.

Ten minutes later, her phone pinged.

"Sorry I fucked everything up and made you feel bad."

Abby almost laughed as she wrote back. "I'm sure you don't mean to trivialize what either of us feels. But 'feel bad' is a ludicrous understatement."

"Well, texting has its limits. How about horrible, bereaved, betrayed, deserted, suicidal, sick, furious, befuddled? At least you can blame me. I feel all that, too, and have only myself to pin it on. Now try to get some sleep."

"I did not desert or betray you," she wrote. "I'm sorry if you feel that way."

"A person can desert and betray himself. Now good night, Bean."

She tried to think of him as dead.

"No texting the dead," she wrote on a Post-it and stuck it on her phone. It worked for a few days.

At some point, Ray must have talked to Walt, because Clarice wrote to her, "Quit texting Ray. He doesn't need to be demoralized by you."

Where did Clarice get the nerve to order her around, intruding into her private life? Abby would never say a thing like that to anyone. She did not write back.

AS THE LONG empty weeks of sabbatical dragged on, Abby was ambushed by memories—not of angry, shouting Ray, but of his real self, the guy he'd been with a healthy heart. He had written poems she knew were secretly about their life, with lines like, "Today there will be increasing clowns and very high humility." Once she found a drawing in her copy of *Ulysses*, of a ladybug and a Sugar Smack, with a heart in the thought balloon of the ladybug and the caption "Love Stinks." He had total recall of every elementary school laugh line, every elephant and knock-knock joke, every pun. When her nieces and nephews were little, they had all spent holidays at Abby's mom's, and Ray liked to sit at the kids' table and make them howl with glee and cries of "Nooooooo," as they begged for more.

In her study was a copy of the Irish Catholic Bible Joyce had used, and one day she noticed an inscription Ray had printed in the front: "Presented to Abigail McCormick on Her Release from Prison"—a joke he must have waited years for her to find. Others he had let her in on right away, like when he tested the search engine on her computer by typing in every possible version of "naked women." No matter how illiterate or abbreviated ("nekkid wimin," "nek wim," "nk wm"), it took him straight to porn, as if the web had been invented just for that.

And then she would recall the, what—ten thousand times?—they had made love. She could still see his perfect Christlike body and feel his silky skin, his energy and passion, his desire to please. He liked to wrap himself around her in the grocery store. He claimed her sweat did not stink. When she cut herself, he expertly bandaged it. He peeled her apples, because she was allergic to something often sprayed on them.

All of that was gone forever now, and that thought left her dazed, unable to function, in a fog of regret.


"SOMETIMES OUR JOB is only to survive," Ray wrote to her, and for a while she took that as her motto. She survived.

But as the fall limped on, she was forced to wake up and notice what was happening in the present. She could not afford her life. Ray was right—she was too broke to ride as much as she had been.

She started to keep track of her expenses and trimmed everywhere she could. She half-leased Beau to a little girl and rode less often herself. She gave up buying clothes and books, giving to charity, and going out to restaurants. Two rotted windows in the dining room had to be replaced, but she put off plastering and repainting the ruined wall beneath. Her ancient refrigerator barely worked, but that also had to wait. She canceled the cable and did without TV. She quit getting pedicures and waxing and haircuts, though she had to color the roots—this was no time to go white overnight.

After a while the vacuum of her life seemed to make room for new friends, in a way her marriage had not. She started hanging out with two professors who rode horses, neither of them Republicans or goons. Ginger was a Cal biologist, a feisty blonde who drove a pickup truck, had been riding continuously since age five, and had never fallen off. She was skeptical of trainers and had a bit of a big mouth, which soon got her kicked out of Abby's barn. But she and her husband lived in Berkeley, and they invited Abby over for pleasant meals.

The other new friend was Nell, who taught French at Columbia and knew Joel. When Joel went to Paris for the school year, Nell showed up in his apartment, on sabbatical. She had ridden in competition as a teenager, and she was excited to see Abby in her boots and breeches in the hall. Nell was a slender brunette, almost as tall as Abby and exactly her size, and Abby lent her gear so she could start taking lessons at her barn. The two of them drove out there together, talking all morning and spending many evenings reading by each other's fireplaces. Nell, like Gillian, was twenty years her junior, but they were instant friends.

It seemed odd that Nell and Ginger did not know Ray, when Abby thought of him as her life, and they were fast becoming her closest living friends. She wished he could meet them, to show him he was wrong about the goon squad at the barn.

And thank God, they were both more supportive than Clarice.

Nell declared, "It would be easier if he had died."

Ginger was more aggressive. "If I ever see the guy, I'm cutting off his legs."

Having friends seemed to make it possible for Abby to go back to work. She wrote more poems, and one afternoon, she typed up envelopes to eight literary magazines. Selecting sheets out of her stack, she thought about what name to use. Poetry editors knew Abigail McCormick was married to Ray Stark, and how they felt about him would color their response, for better or worse, since he made enemies as often as fans. She was tempted to use a young man's name—say, Matt Green, MFA student. The poetry world was very male, and young male poets got lots of encouragement. But she didn't want to create a lie she'd have to clear up later.

Her middle name was Corbyn, her mother's maiden name. In the top left corner of each page she typed A. Corbyn McCormick, added her address, and typed the same onto the return envelopes. The envelopes were fat, and she put on lots of stamps. When she went out for a run, she carried the whole stack to the mailbox up the hill.

COLLEAGUES INVITED HER for Thanksgiving, people she had rarely seen outside the office—but they took pity on her, kindly. It made her see how thoroughly their social life had been Ray's, even with people she had known before she married him, like Sateesh and

Clarice. These days, Sateesh never called, and Clarice only sent her bossy messages.

Christmas week, she tried again with Sateesh and Gloria. In the past, she and Ray had baked cookies and delivered them to friends, wearing Santa hats. This year she wasn't up to cookies or the Santa hat. But she saw a display of blooming Christmas cactuses, bought one for Sateesh and Gloria, and took it by their house.

Gloria answered the door and seemed startled. "I thought it was the UPS man."

She looked like she wanted to slam the door.

But Abby stepped inside and heard Sateesh rattling silverware in the kitchen. "I miss you two. Can I say hi to Sateesh?"

He came out to the foyer, and the three of them stood and spoke stiffly for a few minutes. They did not thank her for the cactus—she slunk away. What on earth were they thinking? Their iciness almost hurt worse than what Ray did.

And for Christmas, Ray sent her a mixed CD of independent rock, produced on the CD burner she once gave him, his traditional present to his friends—as if she had been smoothly translated from love of his life to one of the boys.

# THIRTEEN

TORY'S WHITE POODLE, Emile, snored peacefully beside him on the couch, giving off a faint doggy odor, as Ray sat in his air-conditioned house, feeling like hell. His chest hurt now not only up the midline but all the way into his throat, which felt like it was swelling shut. The night before, it was so bad Tory had taken him to the ER, where they told him fluid was collecting in his torso. The ER doctor stuck a long needle into his chest and drained it, filling a giant syringe with watery orange liquid, like a sick Kool-Aid.

That took the pressure off, and he should have felt better tonight, but he did not. His chest was still on fire, and he was sipping a Bud Light to try to put it out. On the coffee table, the TV showed a Japanese monster movie that was so low-budget you could see the rubber costume on the giant lizard ripple when the guy inside it moved. But that was somewhat amusing, so he watched it with the sound off.

His phone lay next to the TV, and it chirped out the music that was supposed to sound like owl calls but did not. *Johnny*, it said.

He picked it up. "Yeah."

"Just checking in for my nightly dose of cheer," Johnny said. "Hit me with the good news first."

Ray gave him the health report. "Turns out the heart is a sump pump, and mine's not working anymore. Tell me, is it a good thing when people stop saying how thin and pale I am? Floridians used to say it all the time, but now they've stopped."

"Maybe they've gotten used to you," Johnny suggested. "Or you look so bad they're afraid to bring it up."

"Yeah, probably. I'm down to one-thirty."

"Quit bragging. Hey, you should take it easy, man. Eat a steak once in a while and get some rest."

Johnny didn't get it, about his heart, that it was slowly dying in his chest—he thought it was exaggeration, or some kind of metaphor, all in his head. Okay, maybe it was, with all that had happened, with all that he'd gone through, visiting itself on his body. *Psychosomatic* was the word, but nonetheless he could no longer run, could barely swim. He couldn't walk more than a block without stopping to pant. Well, in part that was the weather here in horrid south Florida, where it was hot and humid almost all the time.

Ray changed the subject, told about their dinner a few hours earlier, with a bunch of young wannabes Tory knew from her new job, as a Poet in the Schools.

"Those kids have no idea what to do with me. I'm just old to them. I'm not their teacher, and they don't know enough to be impressed with me. They're like my students. They haven't read a thing."

"Yeah," Johnny said. "Kids today, just ignorant. Same thing Socrates said about Plato, probably."

Ray didn't have the patience to deal with Johnny tonight, and he found a way to get off the phone, just as Tory walked through the dining room. She was ready for bed, in a yellow T-shirt from the Miami Zoo, with lion cubs on it, her lovely slender legs bare below. As he always did, he admired her lithe quickness and grace, and her young, creamy skin, so delicious to the touch—even if she had trapped him into a dinner with a bunch of ignoramuses.

She went into the kitchen, turned the water on and off, then walked toward him, across the dining room, with a small smile— though when she saw the beer in his hand, she frowned.

"You should be in bed," she said, and nimbly plucked it away from him.

He reached to snatch it back, but she danced across the room with it.

"Give that back. It's only nine o'clock. I'm not six years old."

"It's been dark for hours, and you need sleep. It'll help get rid of your chest pain."

"No, it won't. The pain'll keep me awake, so I'm not going in there yet. You go sleep if you want to so much."

She carried the beer across two rooms, into the kitchen—he heard it glug into the sink. Of course she was just trying to take care of him, and she understood better than anyone what he was going through. But pushing him around was not the way—there was something prim about her, like her shining dark hair, cut precisely at the jaw-line and never out of place. But she was just silly about the beer. Of course he could get another as soon as she went to bed.

She came back and stroked the dog's head. Emile lifted his head alertly and thumped his tail against the couch, before he relaxed again with a sigh.

Tory kissed Ray good night, smelling of peppermint from her just-brushed teeth. "Don't stay up too late."

Then she was gone, into the bedroom, and soon the light went out.

Quietly, he fetched himself another beer, eased it open without a hiss, and used the remote to switch to the weather station. It said it was only seventy in Miami tonight, but he knew it would be a wet, oppressive seventy. God, he hated this place.

Eventually the weather station got around to the West Coast, and it was like a punch to his chest. Out there, Pacific storms were sweeping through, power-washing every molecule of air, and in Berkeley every tree and bush would be in such enthusiastic bloom that they would froth over fences, never slowing down.

Yeah, stuff grew that way here, too, but you never got that cold fresh air. It was worth your life to step outside some days, and he hated—hated!—air conditioning, though it was the only way he could breathe. The day he arrived, it had been ninety and raining, and it often seemed like all hell was about to come out of the sky, a hurricane, or at least a violent thunderstorm. Hurricanes in December, for God's sake, flinging cheesy house trailers across the Everglades.

He dreaded the thought of summer, a time he used to love. He couldn't go to Berkeley as a visitor, and he would have to work. Designing and running a new program was turning out to look like year-round work, way more than the department had promised him, in this place where it could be eighty-five degrees in the middle of a summer night. He would have to live indoors and wonder what the fuck he was doing here.

Even now, in the relative cool of winter, his longing for Berkeley hurt like the chest pain—maybe it was the chest pain. That, and the breakup of his marriage. He no longer expected to recover from it, wasn't even sure he wanted to. The pathetic truth was, he had started to suspect the whole thing was a big mistake. Sometimes it seemed impossible that he and Abby had parted, a nightmare. Could he ever get it back, no matter what he did? He didn't know if he could undo enough, if he could ever find a way back or even if there was a back there. He felt like Odysseus, all companions lost.

It struck him that he hated Miami the same way Abby had loathed Morgantown. He had never understood that, how it was possible to hate the place you lived. He checked his phone—she hadn't texted him tonight. Quickly he wrote to her.

"I get it now what it was like for you in Morgantown. I've never hated a place before, but I fucking hate Florida. I'm dying so much faster here. Giving up my California driver's license was a blow. I have a Florida license now, a Florida phone number, a Florida address, like some god-damn ancient retiree. I'm a formerly cool dude, now almost dead."

Within seconds, she replied. "You should go see the cardiologist there again."

"You have too much faith in doctors," he wrote back. "That asshole cardio here? He talked about the heart transplant like he couldn't wait to take a knife to me. They can't seem to do anything else. They can't even explain why I'm still on my feet. According to the numbers I should be in a wheelchair. But I've outlived my dad by seven years, and so what if I can't run anymore. Maybe I should get over the fact that I'm not twenty-seven anymore."

He waited for her reply, so anxiously that he wondered what the fuck he had done to himself. He had thought somehow the better job, and Tory's love, would save him, end the pain, calm everything down. He had never felt such lust for anyone, monstrous because thwarted, when most of his life there had been an easy transit from desire to act, no need for volcanic buildup.

And it had been great at first, living that desire—but of course it didn't last. And now he knew it wasn't going to turn into something better, the way it did for him and Abs, his own String Bean. With Tory, it was just another relationship, flawed like all of them. But it must be worth all he had trashed for it—wasn't it? If it wasn't, nothing added up.

Standing, he paced through his dark house. He did like the place he'd bought. A simple ranch with hardwood floors and exposed beams in the living room, it had a big open kitchen with a bar at one end and tall stools with red vinyl seats. The antiques he and Abby had found around New England looked great here, primitive Shaker stuff—they both had an eye for it and agreed on every piece, surprisingly, given their differences. Out west they collected Japanese *tansus* and old Mexican chests, pieces that went together oddly well and would have looked great here, too—the thought made his chest hurt worse. And the state had required that Abby's name go on the house's title as his wife, though they spelled it wrong (who used *Abigale*?). So it was like she haunted the place. He could see her everywhere.

On the glassed-in porch in back, he looked around the walls for the pink-bellied gecko that lived out there and couldn't find the guy—he must have some hideout for sleep.

Opening the door, he stepped outside—the air felt almost bearable, and he could smell wet dirt. Pale moonlight gleamed on his orange trees, and he walked over to one and put his head into its leaves, inhaling their green, spicy scent, as he felt around for nubby fruit. By day, the trees would be bathed in yellow light and filled with chatty mockingbirds. He did love mockingbirds, the way they imitated anything they heard—the calls of other birds, but also car engines, lawn mowers, and washing machines. And in the mornings, before the heat become unbearable, he could throw a Frisbee for the dog to leap after across the lawn. Come summer, he would just have to make the best of it, dig up the yard for a vegetable garden. Tomatoes probably loved it here.

He turned and looked back at his dark house. He checked the phone in his hand—no, clearly it was Abby he was waiting to hear from. And that meant he was fucked.

A FEW WEEKS later, on a February night, Tory said cheerfully, "Let's go see more of Florida. We've been here for five months, and we haven't left the city limits. Let's go see the Keys. They're only about twenty miles away."

Ray was disoriented enough, just being there, and wherever he was, he never wanted to leave home. But Tory had worked hard to take care of him, and she didn't ask for much. The last few days, the weather had cooled a bit, low seventies by day, sixties at night.

So he agreed, and when Saturday came, they packed the dog into Ray's used Subaru, and he drove them south.

It was beautiful at first, crossing long bridges, low over turquoise water, where sailboats cruised silently and speedboats zoomed along, some headed for the bridge, to zip right under it. Ray kept his eyes on distant objects, hoping to hold off the nausea he could feel threatening. He waited for the vista to open up into wild, clean, empty spaces like where he and Abby hiked. Wasn't some of this national park?

But it did not. The bridges were all clogged with cars, never breaking free, and each island they came to was paved and covered with houses, some in the distance looming large, others in small villages encrusted with signs for tourist restaurants, local museums, gift shops, and ice cream stores.

They drove for hours and stopped for lunch at a funky place on the water that fried everything. While Tory ate shrimp and calamari, Ray managed a few clams and a cup of coleslaw, and gave the rest to the dog.

When they set off again, Tory drove. He and Emile hung their heads out the windows, wind in their hair, smelling salt air and some sort of rot that was half fish, half fruit, scented with diesel fuel. After a while, the carsickness arrived for real.

"Let's stop somewhere," he gasped. "A beach. I need to get out."

It took her a while to find one, and when she did, it was so crowded she had to search for an empty parking space. As soon as she stopped the car, Ray and the dog burst out, Emile tearing off into the crowd of families with towels and umbrellas covering the sand—Tory grabbed the leash and ball thrower and took off after him. Ray leaned over, hands on knees as he breathed deep, trying to stop the nausea.

In front of him was a pile of trash scattered around a bin, sandwich wrappers, red Coke cans, half-eaten ice cream cones plopped on their heads, being explored by wasps, cigarette butts all over them. Once on a ferry crossing to San Francisco, he and Abby had met a man visiting from Florida, who had effused to them about the cleanliness of the water in the bay.

"Y'all keep it real nice here," he said, and flicked his cigarette butt over the side—Abby had wanted to strangle him, though of course she was too polite. And now here was Ray, exiled to the trash heap the guy came from.

He straightened up and searched the crowd—Tory was far down by the water, pitching tennis balls for Emile, who streaked after them joyfully, though he usually failed to bring them back. Ray got his swim goggles and a towel from the car and picked his way through the crowd.

When he got closer, crowd to his back, he could see the beauty here, the turquoise water with gentle waves, shining in the sun. Tory looked lovely, too, trim and leggy in shorts, laughing at the big white dog, as she ran to grab the balls away from him, toss them again.

But down here by the water, there was not a scrap of shade, and the sun was intense, too low, hinting at its lethal side. Maybe the water would be cool at least, and Ray had his suit under his jeans. Whipping the T-shirt over his head, he kicked off his running shoes, dropped his jeans, and waded in, as he strapped the goggles on, to keep his contacts in his eyes.

The water felt cool at first, but when he sank into it, swam a few strokes, it seemed to be the same temperature as the air, or his skin—he couldn't feel where he left off and the water began. Stopping, he made sure he could still touch bottom, caught his breath—he needed those pool rails to hang on now. Afraid to get beyond his depth, he swam parallel to shore, standing when he needed to, feet on the rough bottom—it didn't feel like sand, more like crushed coral. The water was fairly clear, but he couldn't see any fish, just a lot of little kids wriggling past in water wings, small chubby legs churning.

He heard something, high engine whine, more than one, headed his way—it sounded like a gang of motorcycles, or a flock of huge mosquitoes. Lifting his head in time, he saw three Jet Skis bearing down on him, young men on them, one with a girl in back of him, one with a pit bull in front.

"Hey," some dad shouted nearby, and grabbed his kid as the skis roared past, not slowing down, two of them on either side of Ray, swamping him with spray and waves.

The pitch of the motors changed, got higher, and he turned to see the Jet Skis scramble, circle, and change places, before they charged back toward him. One of them—the one with neither dog nor girl—steered straight at him and seemed to speed up. Taking a breath, Ray dived as deep he could and heard the thing churn over him. Something nicked his calf.

He waited a few beats but didn't have the breath—he needed air. He surged up, saw the skis circle again and head his way.

But someone screamed, a woman's voice. "Get lost, jerks!"

Tory bounded through the water, fully clothed, reaching for him—behind her, parents dragged their children out. When she got to him, the water was too deep for her to stand and she had to tread, but she seemed as ferocious as a mongoose defending its young.

"Murderous assholes!" she shrieked at the approaching skis.

They hesitated, looped away. One guy gave her the finger and screamed, "Bitch!"

But finally they did buzz off the way they came.

"You're bleeding," Tory said, and grabbed his arms, tried to haul him toward the beach, kicking the water with her legs.

"I'm all right," Ray protested. But his calf stung badly, and when he looked down, he saw something dark feathering into the water around it.

"Come on," she said impatiently. When they reached a depth where she could stand, she put both arms around him, tried to pull him out.

As soon as he left the water and air hit his leg, it felt like a knife stabbing his calf.

"Yow!" he cried. "What the fuck is that?"

"Hush," Tory said, dropped to her knees, and pressed her hands onto the wound.

"Jesus Christ. Fucking place is trying to kill me now. I guess I wasn't dying fast enough for it."

A crowd soon gathered staring around them, no doubt enjoying Tory's wet tank top clinging to her braless breasts, the nipples standing up. Ray tried to block their view with his body.

A strapping, muscle-bound young lifeguard sprinted up with a first aid kit, exuding rude, obnoxious health.

"Don't you worry," he said as he wrapped gauze around Ray's leg. "I called the Coast Guard on those dudes. They won't get away with it."

The fuck of good that did Ray, who was bleeding through the bandage by the time Tory corralled Emile, got him in the car, and drove them to the nearest ER. She had reserved a romantic room in Key West, but when the ER doctor finished stitching Ray up, he just wanted to go home.

She looked disappointed, but he must have been quite pale, because with a little worried nod, she agreed. She drove them back to Coral Gables, picked up Cajun takeout, and took it to their house, a place he never planned to leave again.

The wound took weeks to heal, and when it did, it left a pink cicatrix on his lower leg, like a fat earthworm—his gift from the great state of Florida and further proof of how he had fucked up his life.

IN MARCH, IT heated up again.

One broiling afternoon, he had to spend three hours in a stupid meeting, everyone mad. It was impossible to get his English

Department colleagues to agree on anything—they just wanted to talk, talk, talk, and do nothing. They were mostly fanged serpents in tenured chairs, but Ray had to work with them, as he tried to create a graduate program that made sense, using their courses from the traditional poetry master's program, plus his experimental classes. So far he'd managed to put up a few rickety footbridges, but mostly by doing things without permission, and for that, people already hated him. Sitting there, his chest burned in a new way, maybe from rage. He could hardly get a word in.

"Look," he shouted, breaking through the blather. "We've already got a couple of poor confused grad students wandering around taking courses across this whole train wreck. If we can just off-load a couple of these weird requirements—"

A coughing fit seized him, and he could not go on. Around the table, people watched him balefully, as if his coughs were blows. He left the room to get a drink of water, and coming back, he noticed his face felt hot. Feverish, or maybe just the weather getting to him—it was in the high eighties outside. Or rage. He adjourned the meeting and could barely walk the mile to where he'd had to park the car.

And when he got in, the air conditioning did not come on—it seemed to have died of exhaustion. Driving home was like sitting in a steam room, and he was dizzy by the time he reached his driveway, panting for air, heart racing out of control. Tory would still be at work, and he felt too weak to open the car door. Windows down, he lowered the seat back and tried to catch his breath. Something was boiling in his lungs.

It was at least an hour till Tory came home, riding her bike, in a blue sundress with a full skirt, showing off her narrow waist. He was in such a weakened state that he felt jealous of her healthy legs, pushing the pedals with such energy, and her young, perfect heart. Damn, his chest hurt, never so bad as this.

She didn't see him in the car. She opened the gate, closed it behind her, put her bike in the garage, and unlocked the door to the glassed-in porch. He heard Emile race out into the backyard.

"Darling?" she called inside. "Where are you?"

Finally he managed to raise one hand and press the horn. He had to tap it three times before she peered out of the front door.

"Darling!" she cried, swooping down on him.

His face must have told it all, because she immediately tugged him from the car. His stomach lurched.

"Watch out, I may barf," he groaned as she half-dragged him around to the passenger side, opened the door and flopped him on the seat. "Where are we going?"

"The ER, of course, dummy. I'll get my purse."

IT WAS PNEUMONIA, they said, his fever dangerously high. Soon he was delirious, emerging from vivid Technicolor dreams to see the inside of an oxygen tent. Abby was in every dream, sometimes attacking him, bitter and shrill. Other times he was back with her in Berkeley, his real life. Once he woke up sobbing. The tent refracted everything, but he was aware of people moving through the room, their faces warped and wrong. He felt encased in plastic wrap and had to fight down panic.

As his fever backed off, they let him come out of the tent from time to time, and he could check his phone. Abby sent him a photo of her on the Golden Gate Bridge with Josh and Adam, his favorite Brown students, who had gone out there to a give a reading together, along with Aaron, another former student, all of them young hot-shots now. Apparently she went to the reading and the party after-ward, and the next morning they invited her to hike across the bridge with them, to cure their hangovers. It looked like a gorgeous sunny day, the three young men grinning around Abby, who was as tall as all of them, wind tossing her long blond hair into the air.

"We saw a school of dolphins right below us, underneath the bridge," she wrote. "They were trying to swim into the bay, but the tide was going out, and they weren't getting anywhere. They kept leaping out of the water in the same spot."

Now he really did feel trapped, immobilized in bed, an IV in his arm, in a place he never meant to be, and a life that wasn't his. Why wasn't he out there on that bridge?

When they let him out, Tory drove him home, and it just felt wrong. She should be out in the world, moving ahead like Josh, Adam, and Aaron, not stuck here taking care of him. He had messed with her life, and his own. His life wasn't here, driving past high-rise hotels, as hot rain fell, hurricanes threatening. He should be on that bridge, with the cool Pacific wind in his hair, watching the dolphins leap in place, with Abby and the students who loved him.

When he was well enough to drive downtown, he bought a note-card with a Basquiat on it and printed inside of it.

*Abby,*
*I can't help thinking of us last year, how we could have not split up*
*and what we could have done to stay together, if either of us could*
*have managed it. I don't want to rehash, but much in my mind,*
*well at least enough, proves your ambivalence to me—no blame,*
*just the truth. I suppose you were so hurt, and offended, justifiably,*

*there was no energy there for you to make much of an effort beyond*
*tolerance, which acquiesced finally in my leaving. I love you, Abby,*
*always will, and miss you so much it causes me tears. I am so much*
*in mourning for you and our life, I don't know what to do. I'm*
*miserable here and was just in the hospital. Pneumonia. Enough.*

*R*

When she got the letter, Abby called—he was in class, and it went to voicemail. He listened to it with his head against the cool wall of his air-conditioned office.

"Sweetheart, I'm so worried about you. Is the pneumonia gone? Are you all right now? But listen, I was surprised by what you wrote, I really was." She paused for a while and went on more slowly. "I probably should not admit it, and maybe I'm a masochist or something, because you were horrible to me. But the truth is you don't really need to mourn for us. Because I'd be lying if I said I was completely over your rotten self."

He started to call her back, behind the locked door of his office—but what if Tory dropped by?

He walked outside, into solid heat, across a part of campus where he never went, loud with redwing blackbirds in the trees, the air smelling of hot cement. Sixteen thousand students were just changing classes, on the move, a crowd he could get lost in. He sat on a bench in thin dappled shade and tapped the "Call Back" button, thrilled when Abby answered.

"It was so good to get your call," he said quietly. "Can you really not be over me, after all I've done to fuck us up? I don't deserve it. It humbles me."

"Yes, go figure," Abby said. "All these years you've been driving me nuts, and now I have the perfect chance to get away from you for good. No one would blame me one bit. But what am I doing? Waiting for you to call me back."

He felt himself start to shake. "I want to see you," he whispered.

She didn't answer for a while. "Just break up with the girl. Then we will see."

Ray swallowed hard. Would he have to tell another woman he was leaving her?

His voice was a croak. "My health is so fucked up, it might kill me."

Her voice was resolute. "You should quit or go on leave and come live here. You're always better here."

By the end they were both crying, and they said they would talk soon.

Later Johnny called, alarmed when he found out what was going on. "How can she not hate you? Be careful. She might knife you in your sleep. Christ, you're screwed now, aren't you?"

Johnny didn't say a word about Tory, since he understood the need to get away from live-in women, and he rarely spent a whole night next to his own wife. What he didn't understand was Ray's quest for home, for dinner with the beloved every night. Only which beloved would that be?

At their house in Morgantown, Abby had planted Heavenly Blue morning glories and trained them up strings to the eaves. Now, in Miami, Ray drove to a nursery, bought a packet of their seeds, and stuck them one by one into a patch of rich soil he had prepared beside the house.

It seemed important to make permanent documents now, so he wrote on paper to Abby again.

*Abby,*

*It was great to talk to you. Well, upsetting, but in a good way, I think and hope. Johnny said today how could you not hate me? I wonder too but I will try to find out. I miss you and us every day, our life. Today I planted morning glories in the yard for you. I love you.*

*Ray*

**"LOOK," TORY SAID** one night a few weeks later, as she sliced carrots for salad. "I know you're miserable. I know you may have to go back to Abby. It's all right. I want what's best for you."

Ray was stunned with admiration for her all over again. This girl had moved thirteen hundred miles to live with him, and now she was saying it was fine, he could fling her back? Or wait—was she having second thoughts herself, half wanting to get rid of his decrepit old body? Insecurity lashed him. If she wanted it to end, he couldn't blame her, and he deserved no sympathy.

"Thanks," he managed to say. "It's hard for me to figure out what's misery and what's just my crappy heart. If I could go back to the way I used to feel, I'd be the happiest guy on the planet."

Clearly there were perils still to be survived, arrows he could fire into himself at will. He would have to tread softly, for all their sakes.

Tory had her own room, with her stuff from Montreal, and after dinner she and the dog hung out in there, talking on the phone to her friends, surfing on her laptop, watching her own TV. When she came out she was friendly, a little wary, asked him how he was and could she get him anything. She pretended not to notice he was drinking beer. After a while she went to bed.

He lay on the couch, trying to think, but it was hard with the pain building in his chest. He wished he could run. That used to be when he could sort things out, the sweat, the oxygen wiping his mind clean, sometimes leading to clarity. Something had to give. He couldn't wait to get this part over with. In a year or two, it would all be different. Or he'd be dead. But yeah, one way or another, over with.

Eventually he got in bed, where Tory was already asleep—he felt self-conscious lying there, like it was under false pretenses now. But he would probably feel that way in Abby's bed now, too.

In the morning, he went outside, into the dazzling heat, to check his morning glory vines, now twirling up the strings he had hung for them. They had no buds yet, but watching them grow was strangely comforting. He had also planted tomato seeds, and the shoots were poking up, growing vigorously and exuding a spicy scent if he touched them. All right. He would decide nothing till summer came.

BY THE END of April, the bugs were already big enough to hear over the air conditioning, and one day he saw a bright blue lizard in the yard. Students had changed out of the pajamas they seemed to wear all semester, into their beach gear, girls in skimpy tank tops in class, even the hairiest boys in shorts.

Before school let out, he had a bunch of trained-duck acts to do, reading gigs around the country, plus some local goofball palaver in a suit. He flew off to read in Washington, DC, and Tucson. In Miami, after finals, he gave the commencement address, no less, and the university presented *Death Ranger* to every graduate. At a fundraising banquet for the local Poets in the Schools, he gave the keynote speech.

Such events were harder since the pneumonia—clearly, his

immune system was crashing, and other people were just walking petri dishes, double-dipping at the buffet. "Are you afraid of germs on doorknobs?" used to be a test for paranoia. But not anymore, in the age of AIDS, herpes, and antibiotic-resistant bacteria, when even strong men used paper seat covers in public restrooms and grocery stores gave out free antimicrobial wipes. Salad bars terrified him now, and reception lines were gauntlets of unwashed hands. Could he get a hazmat suit for ordinary life?

Every day now he called Abby, and at her urging he went warily back to the Miami Dr. Death, to see if he had any new tricks. He did. The guy was young, with a Marine's haircut and piercing green eyes, which took on a special gleam as he pulled out drawings of a thing he wanted to stick inside Ray's chest. It was an electrical gadget about the size and shape of a hockey puck, and it would be wired to his heart, to make it work better.

"It will also act as a built-in defibrillator if it stops," the guy explained enthusiastically. "It's an easy surgery, just a few hours, and you'll be on your feet again in days, no sweat. You'll feel better than you have in years. We can schedule it right now."

Ray shuddered, looking at the thing. It was supposed to go just under the skin, up near his collarbone, and he was so thin now, it would stick out like an oversize doorbell. And since his heart never acted as predicted, they had no idea what it might do to him. It could zap him all day long.

"Thanks anyway. I'll see if I can pull myself back up by less extreme measures." He beat it out of there.

Postcommencement, he gave a reading at Harvard, invited by Walt. The night he flew back to Miami, his plane landed just ahead of a giant storm, purple eyes on the weather-station map. Lightning revealed sudden statuary in the dark outside, thrashings of rain. In the morning it was in the low eighties, but it felt benign.

He went out to check his morning glory vines. They were now producing four-inch bright blue blooms that would live only until that night, when they would wither up and die. It seemed important to appreciate each one, and he didn't like to think of the ones he'd missed the day before.

Tory was at work, and he took his typewriter out onto the porch and wrote a letter to Abby on the paint-color sample strips he had used after he bought the house.

Six Heavenly Blues wide open this morning
to the sun. Tiny hard green tomatoes on the
vines. A wheelbarrow full of rain.

And maybe I can get my life with you back
together. Maybe you'll never be able to forgive
me. Maybe I won't be able to forgive myself.
But, Abby, you were my magnetic north for so
long, I'm adrift now, close to the rocks.

I know I'm going to ask Tory to leave, and
that will be horrible since she has nowhere
to go. Certainly I'm not asking you to feel
sympathy for her. I've made this huge mess and
everyone will suffer. I am so sorry.

But maybe one day you'll see this house that
has your name misspelled on the title. And
I'll buy you a snow cone. I love you, always
have, always will.

Ray

He put the strips in an envelope, addressed it to Abby, applied a stamp, and walked it to a mailbox before Tory came home—not to hide, but to observe a boundary.

A few days later, the mailman brought a new issue of *Poetry*. The cover listed people whose work was to be found inside, and one of them was someone named A. Corbyn McCormick. What? Someone with almost Abby's name? He flipped to the poem.

### BERKELEY PERFORMANCE ART

In the park at dusk the very large black man
comes up the dark cliff slope the same way
that I did and sits on the bench where I do
my triceps dips, facing the band of brilliant red
above the Golden Gate, my white female
body prone on yoga mat, crushing the grass, self-
consciously not turning to look, but aware of his
enormous height, the clothes all black, his muscles
double mine, the empty park, the dark. He turns to see if
I watch him, and what must that be like, to make people
afraid because you take a walk? Both of us wear white
ear buds, white wires to phones, and what if that is Bach
in his, he on a research fellowship in music or psychiatry?
I flip over to do push-ups, exuding strength, as I have been advised,
though that did not work for the Central Park jogger, and I hate
it that I think of her. He stands up, walks closely by, glances,
self-consciously snapping his fingers to the music in his ears,
neither of us person to the other, unable to use our common tongue,
though we both understand the transaction that has occurred,
as I move quickly to the bench to do my triceps dips and leave,

and he slowly retreats into the dark—maybe to return
in bright sunlight, tossing a Frisbee for a dog,
to prove something, the same as I.   ·

That sounded suspiciously like Abby's work of the old days, and wasn't that more or less her name? And the shape of the poem, like a vase, like Keats's urn. She had always cared about the shapes. And the prissily fastidious grammar, the *I* at the end instead of *me*—that was his Abby, too.

Excitedly, he texted her. "Criminy did you get a poem in *Poetry* and not tell me? It sure sounds like you. Way to go, Beanie! But what's with the name?"

She wrote back and admitted that she had, but she did not explain the name. Probably she had wanted to see what would happen if she was anonymous and did not use his fame, or her own from her first book.

It seemed like an omen, or the clincher. That night at dinner, he told Tory he was going to California to see Abby.

"I guess I'll look for my own place," she said. She had been offered summer teaching at a private school and would soon be making more.

He felt a rush of fatherly protectiveness. "Take your time, no rush. Wait till you find something nice. And if the rent's too much, I'll help you for a while."

HE FLEW TO San Francisco, feeling extremely quiet inside, calmer than he had been since before Tory. He was completing the circuit he had started two years earlier, betraying Abby with Tory, now Tory with Abby. Or did this act, this doubling back, erase the other one, the errant stray off course?

Abby waited for him past security, in attractive clothes he'd never seen, light summer draperies, her pale hair softly waved and longer than before. She looked thinner, but her blue eyes shone, and they locked onto his from fifty yards away. It was like it had always been for them in airports, since the early 1980s, back when they could meet each other at the gate. Both of them grinned.

He stood in front of her, and she slid into his arms and pressed her lips to his. It felt so right, he just let everything fly from his mind.

They kissed in the airport, in the car. They drove to North Beach and kissed on the street in late sunlight, strolling entwined to the Italian ceramics place, the Grant Street handkerchief boutique, City Lights Books. They were in Vesuvio, Ray with a draft beer, Abby with a White Russian, when Johnny texted him.

"Awk awk, tookie tookie. Called your house and office, no you. Where are you and what are you doing?"

Ray clicked back, "In San Francisco with Abby, making out on street corners."

"Good Lord," Johnny wrote. "Stunning news. Good luck to both of you."

# FOURTEEN

THEY ATE AT the little North Beach bistro where they'd gone for decades, through several changes of management. They held hands and talked of everything except Tory, keeping to a rule they had established long ago, when Ray made her burn the photos, letters, and journals from her former life. Unlike some couples, they did not discuss relationships they'd had with others.

Instead Abby drove him back to her condo in Berkeley, where they made love, tenderly, sadly. Afterward it felt wonderful to her, lying naked with him, his long arms around her, her head in the tender curve of his shoulder, ear to his big heart. His skin had always felt like rose petals, addictive to the touch, though there was less of it now—he was a skeleton with skin. She could rest her fingers between his ribs. He nuzzled his nose into her hair, as he had always done.

She lifted her head to look at him. "You should stay here for the summer. Why go back? The heat down there has made you worse. We could have some fun. We could look for a car for you, or a scooter, so you can get around more easily."

He smoothed his hand up and down her arm. "I wish I could, but I have crap to do in Miami. The place is in such a snarl, it's a miracle I could take this week. But I'll get another one in July. Turns out, if something needs to be done, I have to just do it myself."

"I'm afraid you're taking on too much. You need to rest. Stay for a couple of weeks at least."

He sighed. "I just can't. And I have to help Tory find a place and move out."

Naked, Abby sat up. "She's still living in your house?"

"I can't throw her out. I took her away from her life. She moved there for me."

"But it's time she had her own place. I mean, if you and I are back together?"

"She'll get an apartment soon."

"So you're still living with her."

"I'm trying to take care of her and make this whole thing as easy as possible. She's been a huge help to me. When the pain gets bad, she drives me to school, since I can't park close, and to doctors and the ER when I need it."

He seemed to want to change the subject, and with a sigh, she let him. She settled back down on his shoulder, as he told her about a surgery the Miami cardio wanted him to have, though Ray had refused. She tried to talk him into it, then let it go. As for Tory in his house, she put the thought away. It was an awkward situation but it wouldn't last.

Next day, they took a hike at Point Reyes and ate at the Lighthouse Café. Ray was tired, so Abby drove them home late in the Porsche, his hand on her thigh.

When she parked in their garage and set the brake, Ray said jovially, "What is it with women and hand brakes?"

Abby closed her eyes. "It would be nice if you didn't remind me that you've been with someone else."

He looked surprised. "Oh, sorry. Didn't mean to do that."

"Can't we just erase this year and go back to the way it used to be?"

"That's what I want, too. But, Beanie, it's going to take time."

WHEN HE FLEW back to Florida, Abby phoned her lawyer, called off the divorce. It should have been final already, but for some reason Ray had never returned the paperwork her lawyer sent to him.

"Are you sure?" the lawyer asked. "Are you sure he's changed?"

"I think so. I've known him a long time."

He said he would just put the case on hold, easy to restart if she wanted.

All her friends seemed startled when she said she had taken Ray back.

"How can you do that?" asked Ginger. "You should kill the guy."

Abby shrugged. "I'm not going to kill him, because he's dying already."

How could she explain? He had been her husband for too long to simply stop. They were a symbiotic whole, with its own weird requirements. It wouldn't work for everyone, but it felt right for her.

And with him gone now, she was okay. She was used to having space and time alone, and at least they talked the way they used to, every night on the phone. It was good to share all that had happened, little moments of the day.

Best of all, he no longer ranted about anything. He sounded calm. When he asked to see what she was writing, she sent him a few poems, and he was kind about them, gave her good readings. Most of the ones she had sent out came back with form rejections, but a few magazines had sent acceptance letters, one of which began "Dear Mr. McCormick," though the other editors were more cautious ("Dear A. Corbyn McCormick"). Every time she placed a poem, it cheered her up. Now that it was summer, she walked down to Ray's café on mornings when she didn't have a lesson at the barn.

A month after his visit, she was disturbed to hear that Tory was still living in his house. "Why is she still there? I thought she got a job. When is she moving out?"

"I can't throw her out, Bean. Please be patient. Give it time."

So she couldn't visit him, and they didn't see each other again till late July, when he flew west. He stayed a whole lovely week, with hikes and cooking dinners and seeing friends, exactly as they used to do, like a trip to their real life. One night, after the guests left, he put on music, and they slow-danced in the dark living room.

"Stay for August at least," she begged. "Why go back early? School doesn't start for you till when, almost September?"

"I just can't. I'm sorry. I'll come back as soon as I can."

Finally, late August, he told her he was helping Tory to move out.

"Good. She's going back to Montreal, right?"

He hesitated. "No. She's staying here."

Abby felt a chill. "Why doesn't she go back? She could get her old job."

"She has jobs here, more than one, better than the one in Montreal. She likes it here, and we're still friends. I'm taking care of her, paying her rent."

Abby's voice was tight enough to sprain a vocal chord. "Paying her rent?"

"Yes," he said tensely. "She moved here to live with me, and it didn't work out, but I still have to take care of her till she gets on her feet. It's expensive here, and she doesn't earn enough yet. I owe her that. Besides, she helps me, drives me around."

Abby persisted. "But you have your own car."

He sounded impatient, as if she had forced something out of him. "I've told you, I can't park close to my office, and I can barely walk now, all right?"

Next morning, he texted her. "I'm sorry, sweetheart. But a lot in my life scares me now. Mainly doubting my own abilities, energy, strength, and future of any sort. I love you, Bean. I know how much I've hurt you and I never will stop being sorry. I hope there's enough left of me to make your life better because of me at least for a little while."

She tried to think of Tory as a member of his staff, a little French brunette in a chauffeur's cap. She did not tell her friends that he had lived all summer with the girl, and now she was moving only a few miles away. As far as they knew, that was over, and Abby and Ray were back together, all mended. She didn't want to hear what they would say if they found out, all the things she was careful not to think herself.

SCHOOL STARTED AT Cal, and one afternoon after class, her mailbox held an envelope from a small press that had published books by Ray and Johnny both. Mail often came from the place, ads for its new books—she almost tossed it into the recycling bin.

Then she noticed the address—it was not on a mass-produced mailing label to Ray Stark. It was typed, to A. Corbyn McCormick. The spring before, when she was very low, she had seen an ad for a contest at the press, publication for a poet's second book. So she thought what the hell, took her pile of poems, gave it a title page, and sent it in.

Time slowed down as she tore into the envelope.

*Dear A. Corbyn McCormick,*
*We are very pleased to inform you that. . . .*

She was so excited, she almost couldn't read the rest.

But then she did. Her manuscript—*My Life as a Goat*—had won and would be published in the spring. The second sheet was a contract she had to sign and return, at which time she would receive a check for a thousand bucks, the second half to come when the book appeared. They also asked for a bio and that she make any final changes to the book by the end of the month, so it could go to press.

Suddenly happier than she had been in years, she had an instinct to keep it to herself—Ray's reaction might be mixed. Everyone's might be, a fact she knew too well, from all the times she'd been happy for Ray and Johnny and Pete and Walt and Clarice, but also felt excluded by their success. Besides, it was such a specialized contest, how much of an honor could it be? How many other entries were there, ten?

She felt her own balloon begin to deflate and refused the thought. No, that was what women did, how they undermined themselves. This was an honor, dammit. She took a deep breath and texted Ray the news. Her phone quacked at once.

"You did?" Ray cried. "Oh, my God, Beanie, that's huge!"

Johnny called her next, having heard from Ray. "Hey. Remember who predicted it? I told you years ago, you're too good to be let out on the street."

Giddy, giggling after those calls, Abby sat down with her platinum pen. On the contract, she crossed out *A. Corbyn* and wrote in *Abigail.* Her bio mentioned her first book of poems, the two Joyce books, teaching at Cal and Morgantown, and the magazines where her work had appeared. It did not mention Ray. Maybe she would dedicate the book to him. Maybe to him and Johnny. Or maybe not. For now, she was out of the closet.

EAGER TO SEE Ray's house, meet his new friends, and celebrate her news, she flew to Miami twice in September, working around her teaching schedule. His house was in an old, pleasant neighborhood, where red geraniums spilled out of window boxes, pink bougainvillea heaped over trellises, and tall, ivy-covered trees formed canopies of shade over the streets. But even with the shade, it was so hot and humid she had to run at dawn, and they lived sealed in the AC. Ray was far too pale, and his skin had a translucent look.

"You're not still dieting, are you?" she asked anxiously, as she watched him eat six raw almonds for breakfast. She pressed a hand over his heart. "Maybe you should let the guy put that thing in your chest. It might make you feel better."

His face closed. "I'm not having any fucking surgery. I feel all right."

They saw no one socially while she was there, though they were not exactly hiding in the house—they went out to dinner several times. They just didn't run into anyone he seemed to know.

But she didn't need to mark her territory. She was there now, rubbing out Tory's fingerprints, leaving her own. Now that she had him back—and a book of poems coming out—she felt generous toward the girl. On one of her visits, Ray was taking care of her poodle, and

Abby took him with her when she ran, his long legs bounding along beside her. She liked Emile, who had fluffy white hair on his ears and such an intelligent face he almost looked human. She was glad to have made peace with the dog at least.

One October night, she was in Berkeley, when Ray fainted in his kitchen in Miami, and Tory took him to the ER. He didn't call Abby till he was back home.

"I guess I need to let them do the surgery," he said. "I don't want that damn thing in my chest. But if it makes my ticker work better, it might be worth it. The pain's been horrible this week, and then there I was out cold on the floor."

Abby was terrified. "And then you just woke up?"

"Luckily I had the phone in my pocket, and Tory got here fast."

Cold sweat broke out all over Abby, at the thought of him passed out, alone. What if he had barfed and aspirated it? "I think I'd better go on leave and come live with you."

"No, don't do that," he said quickly. "This was just a fluke. I worked out too hard this afternoon, and I got light-headed. They gave me something for the pain. In fact, it's knocking me out. I need to sleep. All right? I love you, sweetheart. Good night."

Abby was trembling when they hung up, still scared. Of course, a year and a half ago, she'd been a candidate to inhale vomit, lying in the hall outside Joel's door, and somehow escaped. But she didn't like to think of him there, vulnerable and alone.

Next night on the phone he sounded truculent. "So, did you tell Jacob he won't have to wait too long? I'll be dead soon."

"Sweetie, I don't even talk to him anymore, or not much, just politely in the halls. We have department meetings together, but that's about it. Did you schedule the surgery?"

"Yeah," he said gloomily. "Day after Thanksgiving."

Warmth rushed in her chest. "Oh, I'm so proud of you for doing that. And that's good timing, since I can be there."

He sounded startled. "What? No, don't come. You don't need to be here."

"Of course I do. I want to take care of you. My husband's having surgery, and besides, it's Thanksgiving. This year I'll get there. Oh, and if Tory's going home over the break, tell her I'd be happy to take care of Emile while you're in the hospital."

He was not enthusiastic, but he didn't try again to stop her coming—though when she asked if the poodle would be there, he said no.

"Tory isn't comfortable leaving him with you, sorry. She's boarding him."

Abby was mildly disappointed—she liked the dog. But Pete had said Tory was prickly, so all right. Let her put the poor guy in a kennel instead.

She flew to Miami, and they made a modest version of Thanksgiving dinner for just the two of them, a turkey breast with mashed potatoes and gravy, Brussels sprouts, and Abby's cranberry sauce. Ray had to be at the hospital at seven, and they went to bed early, Abby stroking his bare chest, wincing to think what would happen there in the morning.

In the dawn light, she drove him there, and Ray directed her to the front door. "Just drop me off. They said no need for you to come till noon. I'll be out of it till then."

She drove back to his house and ran. Parts of his neighborhood were slightly wild, with streams in gullies. It was so early still, she surprised an armadillo prowling garbage cans—it was cute, with armored sides and a humble, bumbling walk. She didn't know they lived in Florida. She'd have to ask Ray if he'd ever noticed them.

After a shower, she opened her email. Kathryn, one of her grad students, was trying to file her PhD dissertation that semester, and the deadline was Monday. Kathryn sent her a revised last chapter, and Abby read it, clenching her jaw. It was still a mess.

But she was too restless to wait till noon. At eleven she sent a critique to Kathryn and drove to the hospital. Ray wasn't in his room. She asked a nurse.

"He's in recovery," the nurse said. "The surgery went fine. Are you his wife?"

She wished she had worn her wedding ring—but they hadn't talked about putting them back on.

Finally they wheeled him in and lifted him onto the bed, his long pale crucifix-like limbs too thin and light. He was unconscious, and she pulled a chair to the end of the bed and sat stroking his big wedge-shaped feet through a thin flannel blanket, like the ones she'd worn home from the ER in a cab. He had always slept with his lids slightly ajar, and she could see his big, pale blue irises roll slowly side to side.

After a while he opened his eyes. "Sweetheart!" he cried. "I'm so glad you're here! I can't wait till we can make love again!"

Abby laughed, happy and surprised.

He seemed normal right away, vigorous and cheerful, sitting up in bed, the left side of his chest swaddled in bandages under the thin gown.

"Can you tell the difference?" she asked. "How do you feel?"

He seemed to listen to his heart. "Okay, I guess. Ticker seems pretty steady."

Sitting by the bed, Abby called their friends to say the surgery went well. She knew she was doing it in part to demonstrate that she was there, she was the wife again, she, the only one in the room with him, all of them waiting to hear. She called Johnny, then Pete, since both had often acted like her friends. She called Walt, but not Clarice ("They will have kids, Abby") or Hank ("Don't tell your wife"). But she did call Sateesh and Gloria, who seemed suddenly to answer their home phone. In fact, they both got on the line, quietly asking questions, grateful for the call.

"Everyone sends their love," she told Ray when she was done.

With a look of concentration, he picked up his phone and started to type.

"Who are you texting, sweetie?" Abby asked.

"Tory," he said, not pausing as he wrote.

"Why are you writing her? She doesn't need to know."

"Yes, she does. She was my caretaker all last year."

After he sent the text, she sat beside him, careful not to disturb the tubes and wires hooked up to him, and held his hand. "That was so sweet, when you woke up and said you couldn't wait till we could make love again."

He gave her a blank look. "I did? I don't remember that."

She laughed. "Of course, you were on morphine. Well, it was still nice."

And it was still him, even on morphine, wasn't it? It nagged at her slightly. Would he have said the same to Tory, if she was sitting there? Maybe that was why he called her *sweetheart* instead of *Bean* or *Abby*.

But no, before the split, on email, he had called Tory *darling*, while she herself was always *sweetie* or *sweetheart*—and *sweetheart* was what he'd said. Clearly he knew who she was. She held on firmly to his hand.

# FIFTEEN

let him out, though he felt as frail as a snail without its shell. The bandage had been removed, and now he could see the thing they'd put in him, just as huge and ugly as he'd expected, sticking out from his thin chest, under the skin above his pecs. So now he couldn't even kill himself, because the fucking thing would shock him back to life.

He had to ride a wheelchair to the parking lot, but as soon as they got there he stood up and climbed into the car. Abby drove him home and helped set him up on the couch, with a book and his small TV on the coffee table, everything within easy reach.

"Can I do anything for you?" she asked from time to time.

"You can take this thing out of my chest."

"Oh, sweetie, don't say that. Give it a chance. You're still postoperative, but it's going to be all right in a few days. You're going to feel better."

Easy for her to say—it wasn't in her chest.

And what the hell was she doing? She kept going back to her

laptop, on the bar, two rooms away, across the expanse of dining room and the big kitchen. She faced him but kept her nose in the computer, sometimes printing something, reading it, going back online, using the wireless service Tory had installed against his wishes the year before.

"Can't you at least come sit with me?" he asked, next time she came in.

"In a bit. I've got to get this student thesis pulled together. She has to file it tomorrow, and it's still a mess."

She never did come in to sit with him. But at least she paused long enough to make chicken soup from scratch for dinner, because the stuff had seemed to have healing powers in the past. They ate it with crusty bread, sitting on the red vinyl stools—he had moved his small TV to the bar, so there was basketball in the background. Cautiously Ray sipped a beer, though Abby wasn't drinking anything.

"There's white wine if you want," he said.

She shook her head. "I've cut way back. I might have a nightcap later on."

"And no more pills?"

"Oh, no. I kicked those, what, a year and a half ago? After that fiasco in the hall, with Joel, and the night in the ER. That was your basic wake-up call. If I'd kept going like that, I'd be dead now, or at least in rehab. Better to suck it up myself."

His chest felt spangled suddenly, as he looked at her—for a moment she seemed to be her fine young self again, that tall pretty girl in the pencil skirt, with the dazzling credentials, the book on James Joyce. She was so brave and strong, ready to gallop off a cliff, it seemed like she could do anything. In Berkeley she still had a surf-board in the basement and a horse to ride flying over jumps. She had never dived out of a plane, but she certainly could have, maybe even now—at sixty-two. She didn't look it, not a bit. And she had flown across the country just to be with him for a few days, while he was grouchy on the couch. He felt a rush of warmth.

"Do you need money?" he asked.

She looked startled. "Well, yes, I always do now. Just paid the wretched property taxes."

Oh, yeah—he remembered those Berkeley taxes. They were really steep, to support outstanding schools, shelters and free clinics, bicycle boulevards and pedestrian walkways. The socialist city council had to contend with a high-crime city that had an upscale population in the hills, gangs in the flats, a massive, flammable park on the backside of the ridge, thousands of homeless people sleeping in parks, and even more college students wandering around oblivious on their smartphones, asking to be mugged. It was a bit of a nightmare, but just the thought of it made him ache to be back there, to be part of the place.

He wrote her a check for a thousand bucks.

"Early Christmas present," he said, tearing it out.

"Wow, thanks, sweetie." She kissed him, before she went back to her laptop.

He returned to the couch.

HE WAS SUPPOSED to rest for a few more days, and he had scheduled his Monday seminar to come to the house, seven fine young men who wanted to write experimental poetry. Abby whipped up a batch of oatmeal cookies for them, but said she would go to his office to give them space and continue to help her student from there, with hours yet till the filing deadline in Berkeley.

When the guys showed up, she was still there, probably deciding which of the six pairs of shoes she'd brought to wear—she had altogether too many moving parts. He was sure she'd brought at least three pairs of glasses, too (reading, distance, sun).

He was standing in the kitchen with his students when she came in to say good-bye. It was warm out, and she had on a pink linen shirt, skinny white jeans, and wedge-heeled espadrilles. She gazed around at them expectantly, her smile too bright.

"Hey, you off?" Ray said. He turned to the guys. "Um, this is Abby."

"Hi," they all said shyly.

Abby seemed to freeze, a stricken look crossing her face.

"Have a good class," she said quietly, and rushed out the door.

Of course, of course, he should have said my wife, Abby—Abby, my wife. It was a last-minute failure of nerve—most of these guys had seen him with Tory all the year before.

"Here, let's sit at the dining table," he said, and gestured to it. "My wife and I found it on Cape Cod. It's a harvest table. Oh, and my wife made cookies," he said, and passed them around.

He found a couple more opportunities to mention her as the class went on, and every time he called her *my wife*. If only he had said it with her there, he could have headed off what was probably coming.

It was going to be Abby's last night there, but she stayed away till late afternoon. When she did show up, she brought home groceries and a bottle of wine, which she immediately opened, poured some in a glass, and drank while she cooked. She still seemed upset and unusually quiet. He knew why, but he wasn't going to bring it up. Maybe it would just blow over, and in a few weeks he could go home to Berkeley for Christmas break, everything fine.

She had gone to the best fish market in Miami, and for dinner she made his favorite fish soup. They ate it at the bar, again with basketball in the background. The air was tense, and he found it easy to toss back several light beers, while she seemed ready to ignore her new rules, pouring herself more wine.

Finally, after they ate, they were still sitting on the bar stools when she started to cry quietly. "Why didn't you tell your students that I'm your wife?"

"I know, I know," he said quickly. "You should have heard me in that class. I said 'my wife' this, 'my wife' that. 'My wife always says,' stuff like that. I couldn't stop saying it. I just didn't say it when you were there. I clammed up, because my private life is none of their business. Then I tried to make up for it, but you weren't there to hear."

That was the best he could do right now.

She seemed to be taking deep breaths, trying to calm down. "I think it's time for you to stop paying Tory's rent."

Yeah, yeah. He knew that's what she thought. He sighed.

"She can't support herself yet. But she's applied to go back to grad school at Harvard, and I wrote a letter for her and talked to Walt, so she has a good chance. And when she moves there, she'll be on her own. That'll be the end of it."

It was what needed to happen for her, to help her career, and if she got into Harvard, Ray would be the first to cheer for her. It would be tough for him in Miami without her, but it was the right thing, and somehow he'd get by.

And he was going to be close to Tory forever—they had a bond. If Abby wanted to be around, she needed to understand that, too. It had to be a condition of any reconciliation between them. He should make that clear.

With terrier-like persistence, she went on. "But that's what, nine months from now? That means she'll stick around here and let you support her and take care of her dog and God knows what else, while I'm thousands of miles away? The only way I'll be able to take that is if we put our wedding rings back on and recommit. I mean, we're back together, aren't we?"

So, she wanted to push it to the brink. She couldn't just let events resolve themselves in a natural way. He felt his face get warm, a true sign of better heart health, he supposed—he hadn't flushed for a long time.

His jaw was tight. "I thought we were just thinking about getting back together."

Abby stared at him, eyes wide, face pale. "After all the flying back and forth to see each other? After making love, and sleeping together whenever we can? You don't call that back together? You gave me a check last night."

His face got hotter. "Yeah, and you've done nothing except stare at your email the whole time you've been here, and now you're taking off again. You showed up just long enough to get a thousand bucks out of me."

Abby sprang off her stool. "You said that was my Christmas present. Now you want it back? As for the email, I have a job to do, and it was urgent. This poor kid Kathryn has been doing slave labor at Stanford, teaching comp for almost nothing, but if she managed to file her thesis today, she'll get promoted to lecturer. I couldn't approve it the way it was, and I had to work all weekend to get it into shape."

So her students were more important to her than he was—check. He stopped looking at her and stared at the game on TV.

But she went on haranguing him. "And all this time, you let me think we were back together, when you were, what—are you stringing Tory along, too? After I had the decency to forgive you and take you back, give you another chance, you're keeping the girl in play? After twenty-six years, I'm still auditioning to be your wife?"

He wasn't going to answer that. She was so entitled, so above him, like her Porsche, and the pricey condo in Berkeley, and her horse, and her belief that all the money was hers. He was finally earning something, and she wouldn't let him keep it.

He had a vision of her suddenly, from those three days when she left the house with an air of martyrdom, leaving him to pack, exactly how, when he had no car? As for where she went, he didn't want to know. Christ. He couldn't trust her anymore. What had ever made him think he could?

Her voice was tight, insistent by his ear. "I can't take it anymore, Ray. It's too much. If you won't even say we're back together, that's the end."

Hah! Now she thought she could decide, that all the things were hers and all the money and the decisions, too. She thought she could tell him what to do. Well, that was at an end, for sure, whatever else happened. He was no longer taking orders from her.

She went to pack her suitcase for an early flight, and after a while he realized she had gone to bed. Fine. Let her throw stuff in his face and walk away, feeling no doubt self-righteous and wounded—as if everything was always about her! Had she even noticed that he was postsurgical? There she was, flying in like Florence Nightingale, and what exactly did she do for him while she was here, except take his money and put the screws to him?

He waited till the game was over and he was pretty sure she was asleep or faking it. He went in and lay next to her, not touching.

So another frozen night like this, another woman unhappy next to him. Why did this keep happening? Desire was the problem—the Buddhists understood that. It got you into trouble, and it didn't last. With Abby it had lasted quite a while, but not as long as the results, which were starting to look eternal. At least with Tory he had headed off the eternal part. Hell, he was too sick now to want anyone.

At least the pain pills knocked him out. He slept.

It was still dark when Abby's alarm went off, but he got up, too, and flipped on the ceiling light. He walked into the kitchen to make tea and came back with her mug, just as she was pulling on her jeans, her breasts still bare, exposing the slight softening of six decades, even on her thin frame.

Standing still, he took her in, not saying anything. Could he give up those lovely breasts? So familiar, worshipped so many times, but now fuller than they used to be, and aimed more toward the floor. Maybe if he concentrated on breasts exclusively, he could get through this horror show. Tory's breasts still young, the breasts of his girl grad students exposed in tank tops even in winter, here in Florida.

Abby stared at him accusingly.

"What?" she gasped, snatched up a bra, and quickly put it on.

He left the room without saying anything.

When he drove her to the airport, she said, "If you let me leave like this, you're taking a chance you might never see me again. You know that, don't you?"

Another demand—the hell with that. He wasn't going to cave. Silently, he stared out the windshield of the Subaru. Soon she got out and walked away, dragging her six pairs of shoes in an expensive floral wheelie bag.

* * *

**SO NOW HE** was alone, with a robot in his chest, ready to electrocute him back to life. He felt like Frankenstein or a pathetic inverse Terminator, enacting no deaths but his own. And that didn't seem far off. What happened then? If he saw a bird, a dog, a cat, he wondered if they thought the same. Did they know they were going to die? Did they think they had eternal life, or that death was all there was?

He went through the motions, pretending to live. He didn't talk to anyone. Some days the chest pain crippled him. But the fucking box did give him a bit more energy. He could park his own car now and walk to the office. He could swim more than one lap in a row, though seldom more than two or three.

He had no plans to think of anything except his work. Maybe he'd write another book before he went, one more attempt to show the world that poetry was more than rhyme and jiggety-jog meter. Fuck Pete, who thought what he and Johnny wrote wasn't poetry because it was not enslaved to the metronome. Johnny saw things in the world that no one else could see. He had brilliant, precise perceptions that were unforgettable. He, Ray, could only hope for that, and try for a few laughs, then light the whole thing on fire.

For Christmas, Johnny drove the couple hundred miles down from Gainesville, Sarah off in Africa on a volunteer mission with a French medical group. He stayed a week, and the two of them banished Christmas entirely, joked about the Festival of the Baby Cheeses, the mysterious star over the dairy counter, and a grudge match between the Easter Bunny and Rudolph the Reindeer. They saw monster movies, played pool in bars, ate Cajun barbecue. They argued about poetry, and whether words could or should try to represent reality, and if personality was fixed or every bit in flux. In Johnny's view, divorce was a good thing, and Ray should do it fast.

"Move on to the next thing. Think of the possibilities, the beautiful unknown. You'll be a different person in a year."

"I'll be dead in a year," Ray said.

"Aw, cut it out. Look at you, you're fine. Just get those divorce papers in."

Ray didn't have them anymore—he threw them away the day they showed up, over a year ago. Fucking nosy lawyers wanted to know every detail of his finances, and it was none of their business. If Abby wanted a divorce, let her figure it out. He wasn't going to help. And Johnny could go fuck himself for not believing him about his impending death.

After he left, Ray gradually sank back into the misery of serious chest pain, with new shortness of breath and declining strength, as if the hockey puck was already giving up. What next, let them rip his heart out and patch in a stranger's, so his body could reject it forever? They'd have to shoot him up with the kind of drugs they used to give Abby and crush his immune system. He'd have to live like the Boy in a Bubble, or risk getting pneumonia again.

And he had never reacted as expected to any treatment. He had done better than predicted for the last ten years on nothing but blood-pressure drugs, and now he had submitted to the surgery that was supposed to make him feel so goddamn much better, and he sure as hell did not. He wanted to take a kitchen knife and dig the thing right out.

One sultry January evening, he was feeling low when his phone went *ping,* Abby checking in with an update on his awfulness.

"I just feel so rejected by you," she wrote. "How can you not care about me at all now? The way you looked at me that last morning, like I was a piece of meat. It was so cold."

Rage shot out of his fingertips.

"Don't play the victim with me," they tapped out. "Did you ever once think about what the last few years were like for me? I've been dying right in front of you, and you never noticed. You were too busy riding your horse."

*Ping* went his phone again, Abby writing back. Couldn't she just shut up?

At least Tory was still friendly, when she checked in to see how he was. Sometimes she flirted with him, sometimes she was a bit distant, reserved. Once he saw her leaving a café, in a yellow sundress, slender pale legs gleaming, small feet bare in sandals, and he thought, *Damn, that's an attractive girl*, before he noticed who it was. Well, she was an attractive girl. But it had not worked with her, and he had messed with her enough—he would be expiating that for years.

He was the Monk of Miami, tormented by demons in his chest, on the way to martyrdom.


IN FEBRUARY, HIS heart started swooning every now and then. Sometimes he thought it was about to stop pumping, but it jerked back to life, wriggling like a handful of tadpoles. Every time it happened, he felt like a ghost, a shade, watcher from shadows.

Miami Dr. Death ordered an echocardiogram. His ejection fraction was twelve percent.

"Won't be long now," the green-eyed doc said cheerfully, and put him on the transplant list. "We'll get you on there now, so by the time you need it, you'll have some seniority. You'll be getting close to the top."

Nothing had ever depressed Ray as much as that. He had no idea what he would do, if they tried to crack open his ribcage and remove his heart. Would he let them mess with him that much? Even if the transplant worked—a long shot, he was sure—what would that recovery be like? Six months in the hospital, by himself, alone, and would he ever be the same again? Surely better just to die quietly, especially if he was unconscious and didn't see it coming.

One afternoon he was in the local organic grocery, trying to find anything he wanted to eat, when the blood drained straight out of his brain, like someone pulled the plug. He woke up on the floor, unknown Floridians gazing down at him.

Tory must have been in the store, too, unbeknownst to him, because suddenly she elbowed through the crowd, in the yellow sundress, and knelt next to him.

Instantly she took command. "I know him. He has a heart condition. Please dial 911." She gave them the name of his cardio, to tell the dispatcher.

To help him breathe, she undid the top buttons of his shirt. She started to cry, silently, not asking for attention, just tears sliding down her cheeks.

He squeezed her arm. "I'll be okay. This has been happening lately."

But he held on to her hand, and when the paramedics came, they let her climb into the ambulance. It seemed to steady his heart, just touching her.

It was already dark when they released him from the ER. Both their cars were still back at the organic grocery, and he called a cab to take them there.

But instead of going to her car, she climbed into his, and he drove to their favorite restaurant from the year before, an unpretentious

Cuban seafood place, brightly lit, with a dance floor, live band, and local fresh fish. He wasn't hungry, but it was good to sit beside her in a wooden booth.

After they ordered, he was overwhelmed suddenly by Tory's presence, the warm sweet smell of her hair, the pulse he could see beating in the tender skin of her neck. He loved the eagerness in her face as she looked around, watching a pretty waitress dance with customers between orders, two-stepping, short skirt swirling to show off a slender waist and pretty legs, almost as nice as Tory's own. They had often watched her the year before.

"She's still here," Tory said happily, tears dried now, leaving salt tracks on her cheeks.

Why had he denied himself this simple pleasure, sitting with her in a restaurant, holding her hand? It was like he'd sent himself to hell. Well, maybe he had done his time. Maybe now he could be with her and get the demons to leave him alone.

"I've missed you," he said, realizing it was true.

Tory studied his face. "You're not going back to Abby again, are you?"

He shook his head, though it made him sad. "No, I don't think so."

Gracefully she slid one small arm around his waist and pulled him close against her taut body.

"Good," she said. "Because I'm coming home with you."

# SIXTEEN

ABBY KNEW SHE and Ray were not like other couples, any more than his heart was like other hearts or his mind like other minds. It didn't matter what they said in the heat of the moment. It wouldn't even matter if they got divorced, and in December, when she came back from Miami, she had restarted the process, just to straighten out who owned which house and simplify their taxes—though she heard nothing from her lawyer after that for months. But Tory had gotten into Harvard, and once she went, Abby knew he would stop feeling guilty and come back to her, because he always had before. She could give him time.

And they were still deep in conversation, texting every day, about little things and big. It was the same relationship he'd had with Tory before he lived with her, and now he was having it with Abby. Surely it was going to lead somewhere.

"I'm seeing Tory again," he mentioned in March. "It's nice to have someone to go out to dinner with."

Abby knew he meant that's all it was—"seeing" someone meant

just that, not sex. It was a misunderstanding they once had, back in Morgantown, when they first started going out. He told her he sometimes saw the girl in the pink angora hat, and with her Berkeley instincts, Abby assumed he meant he sometimes slept with her.

When Ray had realized that, he was horrified. "You thought I would just two-time you like that? What kind of jerks do you know?"

So she wasn't worried now. Tory would be gone soon, and it was okay that she and Ray were friends. Abby envied him, having someone to go out to dinner with.

Abby's book came out, the cover design a very cute goat in spectacles, and she flew to New York for the book party and a reading. They were small events, nothing compared to the hoopla that surrounded Ray, the big audiences, other poets showing up.

But several of her grad school friends who taught around New York were there, and Nell took a cab down from Columbia with an armload of white lilies. Afterward they all went to a bar and talked for hours. Her friends wanted to know what was up with her marriage, and Abby explained that they were in a sort of limbo.

"The girl got into grad school at Harvard, and he's told me that will be the end of it, when she goes. He wanted to make sure she was all right and on a better career path. She was his student, after all. And when she's out of the picture, he and I will see. We're still married, technically. He can't seem to face the divorce. He ripped up the papers my lawyer sent him."

Her friends murmured skeptically, most of them with marriages that were more conventional, husbands at home right then with the kids. But she did not try to convince them, and they went on to talk of something else.

There were things she could not explain to her friends or anyone.

Asleep, in her dreams, Ray was always there. Sometimes they tried to find a place to be alone, so they could make love. It seemed to be something her mind required, and it could be unbearable to wake up to a world where he was not. But if she put her feet on the floor and kept moving through space, she found a way to make it till bedtime again.

In April, she was in Berkeley, impatiently counting off the weeks till Tory left for Harvard, when Ray texted her. "What's taking so long with the divorce?"

Abby was surprised, after all his resistance. "Did you fill out the paperwork?"

"Yes, and sent it back."

She called her lawyer's office, and they said he had returned the second set of papers but didn't fill them out or include his financial documents.

She wrote back to Ray. "They need your bank account and credit card statements."

"Fuck that," he wrote. "None of their goddamn business."

"Hey, it was your idea," she replied. "I didn't want to stop being married. If you can't fill out the papers, get Tory to do it."

After all, Tory was around, helping him, being his nurse, and she was implicated here. Let her help, if Ray wanted to go through with it now.

"No way," he texted back. "It's not her mess. It's ours."

"True," Abby conceded. "All right, send me two months of your pay stubs, credit card and bank statements. I'll get new forms and fill them out."

It was just another of the million small tasks she had always done for him. She helped him spell, proofread his manuscripts, balanced the checkbook, paid the bills, made his doctors' appointments and travel arrangements. She was his interface with the world. He needed her. That was all this meant.

It took him months to get around to it. It was June before he sent the documents, and she went over them. The credit card bills listed charges to a hair salon she didn't know he used, though of course he had to cut his hair. There was also a purchase at a women's clothing store, but he was generous and liked to buy presents. There was a charge from a dog groomer, but he loved dogs and sometimes took care of Emile.

One set of items puzzled her: restaurant bills on the same night, in Miami and Chicago, where she knew Ray had gone to give a reading. Grocery store charges in Miami, too, while he was away. Did he give the girl a copy of his credit card?

She called him up, and it went to voicemail. "I did the paperwork and got the figures they wanted off your statements. But wow, Ray, speaking as your accountant, I have to say, you thought I was bad? That girl is into you for a lot of bucks. I thought you were just going out to dinner with her? Good thing she's leaving soon. Your bank account could use a break."


CAL HAD GIVEN Abby a generous travel grant, and in July she flew to Paris to join Nell, who was over for the whole summer. Nell had lived there for six years, working as a translator, and Abby had heard her on the phone, bursting into rapid French or Italian, as she spoke to friends on the far side of the world.

Now those friends lent Nell places to stay, big enough for Abby, too. After weeks trolling around Paris, they took a train to Tuscany, rented a car, and stayed in a tiny stone village surrounded by olive trees, with an icy swimming hole in a nearby creek. They stayed in a villa on the Tyrrhenian Sea and swam in warm blue water, before moving on to Venice and a top-floor flat with roof-deck that belonged to a Spanish psychoanalyst. They explored little-known canals with tiny shops, avoiding the crowds from moored cruise ships, who followed predictable routes, like ants. They rode the vaporetto, ate wonderful food, and watched men blow glass.

It helped pass the time, while she waited for Tory to go, and Ray to come to his senses. While she was there, he sent reports of his progress. In mid-August, he packed a U-Haul and drove Tory from Miami to Cambridge, where he helped her get set up.

So when it was time to fly back to the States, Abby did so with new hope. She and Ray texted more freely now, since he'd gotten the girl out of his life, in a way he could live with—in a good grad program, far from Whitney Ames. Every time they texted without mention of her, Abby breathed more easily. Tory had poisoned every conversation for too long, and now she was gone.

One beautiful September morning, Abby decided to climb onto the roof of their building. A rare hurricane in LA had caused a rainstorm in Berkeley, and water had cascaded from the gutters, which meant they were filled with leaves. Ray was the one who usually cleaned them out, but she did not suppose there was any trick to it.

The air was super clear, washed clean, as she crawled up the rickety fire escape, carrying a garbage bag. Glancing down from four floors up gave her vertigo, but these days, her balance was good. She was running and riding well, and she felt strong.

When she reached the wide flat roof, the sun was bright, and a panorama opened up—blue bay, San Francisco white on its hill, white fog near the red bridge. She was so high up, it seemed nothing stood between her and Japan.

She had brought her phone, and she took a picture and texted it to Ray. "Great view from the roof. I didn't know. You kept that to yourself."

He instantly replied, "Abby, be careful! I'm calling Joel to help you right now."

"No need," she wrote serenely. "I have on tennis shoes with sticky soles. This is more fun than reading inside on a beautiful morning. How are you feeling, honey?"

"Crappy. Lots of fatigue and pain. Had to go to the ER again last night."

Alarmed, she wrote, "Maybe you need to go somewhere else, get another opinion. Like the Mayo Clinic or somewhere in New York. I'll do some research on heart doctors."

She imagined flying wherever he went, to give him support.

"These guys are all right," he texted back. "They're roughriders. I like their attitude. They don't get discouraged easily. And I'm okay. Teaching, running the goddamn program, making progress with the snakes."

When they stopped writing, she examined the roof. It was slightly sloped, so that water ran to the front corners and into chutes connected to downspouts. But the sycamores along the street were taller than the building now, the chutes easily clogged with brown leaves the supposedly drought-resistant trees shed all year long.

She lay on the gravel in one corner, reached down the chute, and scooped out soggy leaves. When she had gotten all she could, she attacked the one on the other side, filled the bag, and decided to airmail it to the driveway. Standing at the parapet on the roof's edge, looking gingerly over, she waited till no one was on the sidewalk, then let it fly—it sailed for a long time before the *whump*. Feeling like a kid dropping water balloons on passersby, she went down to empty it into the yard-waste bin.

On her way back into the building, she noticed the mail had come, including a thick manila envelope addressed in Ray's printing. Pleased, she sat on a retaining wall by the driveway and opened it.

Inside were the divorce papers. He had signed them and enclosed a note.

*Abby,*
*We were legendary and heroic. We were a love for the ages. I will*
*be sorry forever for what happened to us, and I will always love you.*
*You know that, right?*

*Ray*

Her heart clanged dangerously—that wasn't what she wanted to hear. Nothing so final as that, an elegy for them—surely it was not so certain they were done. There would be another act, as there had always been. They fought, they made up. They broke up, they got back together. It wasn't possible that it could end.

But, yes, they could get divorced. It was just a property arrangement, a legal deal. Refusing to feel anything, she signed the papers, slid them in the envelope her lawyer had provided, walked to the nearest mailbox, and dropped them in.

THREE WEEKS LATER, the papers came back, covered with legal stamps. The divorce had been declared October 1.

"So we're divorced," she texted wistfully, and he wrote back right away.

"Yes, Beanie. I am so sorry I caused you pain. I will be sorry forever."

At least he wasn't with Tory. So long as that was true, and he wrote her every day, there must be hope.

Her right knee hurt, and it was hard to run. She had changed doctors, to a practice in the suburbs east of Berkeley, because the hospitals were better there, and she had a smart woman doctor now. When she went in about the knee, she surprised herself by crying in the examining room.

"You should be dating," the doctor said. "You're still cute. Why don't you take a class? You'll meet someone. You'll do better then."

Her friends all said the same thing, when she talked to them. "Are you dating yet?"

Dating—what a concept. And date who, anyway?

"What about Jacob?" Ginger asked. Ginger's husband worked out at the same gym as Jacob, and he said Jacob's latest live-in girlfriend was gone.

Abby laughed. After all the accusations, it could be twisted revenge. But she could see it only in relation to Ray. She had no desire to solve the mystery firsthand, of why women got close to Jacob and then ran.

No, to date she'd have to find someone she was attracted to, who wanted her, a woman of sixty-three, when every man she knew hooked up with someone much younger whenever he was free—or even when he wasn't. She had read somewhere that a woman was more likely to be struck by lightning than to marry after fifty.

"Go online," suggested her horse trainer, who was on about her twentieth romance from dating sites. Sometimes her current guy showed up at the barn, and two months later, there would be another one. She was attractive and barely forty, but even so she didn't make the process sound like fun: "I'm so sick of myself, I could die," she had told Abby, about all the dinner dates, selling herself, how wonderful she was.

And Abby was pretty sure it would be worse for a woman her age. She rode with two reasonably good-looking women in their fifties, Bunny and Jennifer, who had tried it. One morning after a jumping lesson, she went for a trail ride with them. As their horses ambled on a dirt road past live oaks and fields of tall green grass, Abby asked them how the dating was going.

"Christ, they're all such losers," Bunny said. "They lie about their ages."

Jennifer agreed. "They never use a current picture. You meet the guy, and his supposedly black hair is white. Or he's bald, and he has a huge potbelly."

"And if you meet one you like even a little bit?" Bunny said. "He'll never call you back. Even the fat bald ones don't usually, after they meet you for coffee, because they all want a woman twenty years younger than they are. I'd have to go for a guy who was close to eighty, and I could end up being a caretaker for a virtual stranger."

Jennifer turned in the saddle and looked at Bunny. "But you had a boyfriend for a while, didn't you, that cherry farmer in the San Joaquin?"

"Oh, yes, and he broke up with me in a text message. He also claimed to be sixty-one, and he was in his seventies. His photos were about twenty years old."

Jennifer started to laugh. "Last week I was on a coffee date with a lawyer, and he took a call from another woman. He told her he was in a meeting, like it was professional."

"Get this!" Bunny cried. "I saw a profile of a guy who claimed he was fifty-seven, though God knows how old he really was. And how old do you think he said his ideal match would be?"

Abby knew the answer already. "Thirty-six?"

"Twenty-nine?" Jennifer guessed.

"No! Eighteen to thirty-three!"

ABBY WENT TO a knee surgeon and scheduled arthroscopy for a torn meniscus. Late October, day of her surgery, she decided to bike to the hospital, sixteen miles to the east, since she would get no exercise for a few days afterward. Cycling across town, she carried the bike onto a BART train and took it through the tunnel under the Berkeley ridge. Getting off on the other side, she rode east in cool morning air, on paved trails beside canals, past dog walkers.

The surgery was easy, just two quarter-inch incisions, and they gave her the drug that Michael Jackson used to sleep. It burned clean, and she woke up clearheaded after an hour. Ginger showed up with her pickup truck, hoisted the bike into the back, and took her home. Abby was on crutches, leg in a stiff brace, and she had to scoot backward on her butt up the carpeted stairs. She was supposed to stay in bed, but only for three days.

Next morning she was reading, when Ray texted her.

"Bean, I'm in the ICU but doing okay." He sounded normal, and he'd been in the hospital so many times since he went to Miami, she wasn't worried.

"I had knee surgery yesterday, so I'm in bed, too. Want to talk on the phone?" It seemed like they could keep each other company.

"Knee replacement?" he wrote back.

"No, nothing serious, just arthroscopy. I'll be up by Sunday."

She heard nothing back. But the pain meds kept her mellow, and she indulged them and slept, till four o'clock that afternoon, when Walt called from Cambridge.

"Abby, Ray's heart has crashed. They've got him on life support. He's been unconscious since this morning, apparently."

Agitated, Abby shot out of bed and hobbled to the living room, where she called Nell in New York.

"Are you going to Miami?" Nell asked right away.

Abby wondered why she didn't think of that—she must have been in shock. She called the airlines, tried to get a special fare, told them it was her husband in the ICU (close enough! They'd been divorced for what, three weeks?). They wanted to know the name of his doctor and the hospital, and she cursed herself for not asking him. Couldn't she have seen this day coming?

She called Johnny's cell—Johnny would know. He might even be there already.

"I'll ask Tory," Johnny said. "Let me know where you're staying when you come. We can have dinner."

Abby choked on the words. "What's Tory doing there? She went to Harvard!"

"She came back. He was just too sick. He needed someone to take care of him."

Outrage flooded her. "Why didn't he tell me? I can't believe he'd ask a stranger to do that, after all these years. He should let me take care of him!"

Johnny's voice was mildly impatient. "What, and drop your teaching job? You know you can't do that, Abby. But listen, I'll ask her who his doctor is and call you back."

All right, fine. She and Tory could forgive each other, think only of what was best for him. She imagined tearfully embracing Tory in the hospital, both of them loving him, and he so close to death.

While she waited to hear back from Johnny, she called the knee surgeon—flying was on the list of things she wasn't supposed to do for a few days.

The surgeon called her back himself. "It'll probably be fine. Just drink lots of water and stay off of it whenever possible. Use the wheelchair option. Roll through the airport in style."

With the focus of a mom about to lift a truck off her toddler, she hobbled to her closet, pulled out a suitcase, and threw clothes in it.

Johnny called her back, sounding bemused and hesitant, which he never was.

"Um. Did you know they were married?"

Impossible. Ray had promised he wouldn't marry her the second they were divorced. And he would have told her, wouldn't he? He would have told!

Her voice had to fight through a series of Houdini locks. "Did you know already? Did he tell you?"

"No. I just found out, from Tory. And, Abby?" Johnny said. "You can still come. Tory knows it's a fucked-up situation. But I have to tell you, she has talked to his doctors and gotten you barred from the ICU. So you won't be able to see him."

AN EAGLE HAD ripped out her heart, leaving torn arteries, lungs sucking air from the wrong end. And yet it was Ray's heart they were going to do that to, and she would not be there. Some girl had barred her from his hospital.

She could not take it in. She was exactly where she had been before he ever told her about Tory, in the dark, prepared for nothing. And he was gone, unconscious, maybe never to wake up.

Johnny sent her an email, misspelling her name as he always did. He put it into lines like a poem.

*Dear Abbie,*
*I am so sorry for your grief and how complicated and paradoxical*
*and tragic all this is. I know Ray loves you and always will love you.*
*Never through the last two years did I hear Ray say anything but*
*that he loved you—through some hard times.*
*That said, I don't think you should go to Miami.*
*You seem too turbulent in your emotions, too full of too many strong,*
     *mixed feelings*
*for it to be useful, either to you or Ray or Tory. And his life is*
*so precariously balanced right now, that the slightest upset could turn it.*
*Of course, you've got to do what you have to.*
*I told Tory that you plan on coming.*

She called Johnny and said, all right, she wouldn't go.

"Why did she do it?" she managed to ask. "Bar me from the ICU?"

Johnny sounded impatient. "Because of all those angry text messages, of course. She assumed you were coming to have some sort of confrontation with him."

She still had Tory's cell number, from the days when it appeared six hundred times on her phone bill. That night, in grief and despair, she sent her a text.

"Tory, I feel for what you're going through. But you have misjudged me if you think I needed to be barred from the ICU. Ray is not good at describing people, and he has given you a scary image of me. I was coming there so that you, Ray, and I could make peace before he dies. And if you wonder why I would do that, there are things you don't understand."

Like that Tory had loved him for ten minutes and Abby for a thousand years. She probably didn't know that he and Abby were still in constant touch. And that Ray had said when Tory went to Cambridge, that would be the end.

Ten minutes later Johnny called, incensed.

"No! You are not to text Tory! Don't do it! No!" he shouted, as if she were a dog he was swatting on the nose with a rolled-up newspaper.

STUNNED WITH DISBELIEF, Abby lay facedown on the couch, weeping.

Walt called from Cambridge. "Tory's sending email bulletins. I asked her to put you on the list, so check and see if you got them."

She checked and called him back.

"No," she whispered, unable to muster greater breath.

"Okay, I'll forward them to you. I'm sorry, Abby."

She thanked him, clinging to that thread, all she was allowed.

The emails came from Walt. In the address box was a long list of people she had never heard of, friends of Tory, she supposed. She herself was not on the list.

As the days went by, Ray was still out cold, machines pumping his blood. From the forwarded emails, she learned that he had been rated 1A for the transplant, top of the line. But when his heart failed, so did his liver and kidneys, which made him too sick to withstand surgery, so he had been downgraded. He needed to recover first.

"He's still unconscious," Tory wrote. "But his color's getting better. He's recovering and getting stronger. They slightly upgraded his rating today. He's at 1B now, still waiting to become 1A. When he gets there, we just have to wait for a match."

One day when Tory was too busy to write, one of her young friends did it.

"I got to see Ray for the first time in here," the other girl chirped, sounding like she would dot the *i*'s with hearts. "And his hair looked great! As soon as he wakes up, I'm going to tell him that!"

Walt sent that to Abby and called her. "Have we turned him over to the kids? He seems to be surrounded by strange teenagers. Is there anyone he actually knows with him?"

"Maybe Johnny," Abby said. But she wasn't checking in with Johnny, since he slapped her on the nose.

Finally, after ten days, her phone went *ping*.

It was Ray. "Awake again and more robotic than ever. Ticker did a belly flop and isn't coming back. So I'm on this damn machine till I get a heart. How's the knee?"

How could he care about her knee? She had already gone for a hike with Ginger, while he was still hanging in the balance, unconscious, almost dead.

She didn't have to think about it—she knew she'd never mention what went on when he was out. The time for complaints was done.

"OMG, I'm so glad you're awake," she wrote. "That was extremely scary, sweetheart! Don't do that again!"

That night Walt sent the latest from Tory. "He woke up today and got moved up to 1A! So now we're in constant surgical readiness, just waiting for a match."

Abby didn't often pray, but now she did, on her knees beside the bed—meanly, selfishly, for a motorcycle accident near Miami and the death of a strong young man with a perfect heart and no helmet.

Walt asked Tory again to put Abby on the email list, but she did not.

So Abby wrote to Ray. "Honey, could you ask Tory to put me on the email list? I need a source of news when you're unconscious. Walt's been forwarding them, but he shouldn't have to."

He did not reply, nothing that could be construed as critical of his new wife. But next day, like magic, she got two copies of the email, one from Walt, the other from Tory.

**WEEKS LATER, RAY** wrote to her that he was still waiting for a match. But they let him leave the hospital, with a portable version of the machine that was keeping him alive.

When he got home, he emailed Abby himself, and often texted her, sounding much quieter than usual. She asked him to describe the machine. Size of a big canister vacuum, he said, and he had to take it everywhere he went, even into the shower, because if he wasn't hooked up to it, he would instantly die. But he didn't call it the fucking machine or the damn device or anything like what he used to say. He didn't curse at all.

"Thing tocks all the time," he wrote. "And the tubes go right into my chest. But it's keeping me alive, so I can't complain."

"I'm praying for a heart," she wrote.

"You, praying?"

"Yeah. It's come to that."

It made her cry, just to get a text from him, any text, because it meant he was still alive. Every day she expected to hear he'd gotten a new heart. Every day she did not hear that. Every day he had to drag around that canister vac.

Walt sent her a link to a new website, set up by Sateesh, asking for donations for Ray's heart transplant. It included a moving essay by Johnny, who told of Ray's accomplishments and the nature of his condition, which he called "hypotrophic cardiomyopathy"—when it was the opposite, hypertrophic, too big rather than too small, though the result was ventricles clogged up with muscle. Had Johnny even asked Tory? Or did Tory have it wrong herself?

Johnny wrote that the transplant would cost seven hundred thousand dollars, and though Ray had health insurance through his job, it would stop far short of that. So he needed money, and fund-raising events were being organized across the country, with major poets reading Ray's work and suggested donations by those who went. One was set for UC Berkeley, organized by the college librarian.

Abby sent him an email. "I was married to Ray for twenty-seven years, until two months ago. I understand his work as well as anyone, and I would love to read from it."

She did not hear back for weeks.

Finally the librarian wrote, "No. The participants have already been set."

Period. Not one word after that. Was it Tory blocking her again? Or Sateesh and Gloria? Did everyone they know think she was evil now?

At least Walt and Clarice were still her friends, and they were flying in to read at the Berkeley benefit. Walt wrote to ask if she was going to be there.

"Of course," she said to that.

But when the night arrived, her flag flew about an inch above the floor, and she knew she would just be a spectacle, weeping, distraught. So she stayed home, though half a mile downhill, people were celebrating the books Ray wrote when he was with her.

Next day, Clarice and Walt took her out to lunch. At close to seventy, Walt was still handsome, tall and dark, and he had courted the beautiful Clarice when his first marriage fell apart. They took her to Chez Panisse and told her about the reading the night before.

Proudly Clarice said, "I read 'Say Cheese,' and I started out by saying, 'This poem is from a book that's dedicated to Abigail McCormick, to whom Ray Stark was married for almost three decades.'"

Walt had also gone to the benefit in Miami, and he described it to Abby. "Afterward there was a party at his house, and I sat next to him on the couch for a long time, but he wouldn't talk to me. It was really strange. I called him several times after that and he never called me back. I sent him emails, too, asking what was going on, why he wasn't talking to me anymore, and he finally wrote back. Know what he said? He said when I was there in Miami, I talked too pointedly about you."

Abby felt oddly humbled by this, sort of shrunken, like she was Thumbelina now. Ray almost worshipped Walt and loved him as much as any of his friends. But he had cut him off simply for talking about her—as if he should not have to be reminded she was still alive. As if his friends had to take a loyalty oath and never speak to her again.

"How did he seem?" she asked in her new tiny Thumbelina voice.

"He's not the same person. He holds himself completely differently, protectively. It's as if he's trying to keep everything extremely quiet, like a loud noise could kill him. And of course he has to drag that machine everywhere. He doesn't even play music now."

Abby was amazed—Ray without music? He really must not be the same person.

Walt had brought along a copy of *Miami Living* magazine. The cover photo was of Ray, looking pale and wan and very young, like a sick teenager, taken on what she recognized as his front porch. But it was a close-up, only of his face, not showing the vacuum cleaner or the tubes attached to him.

Inside was an interview with him and Tory Grenier Stark, the heroic young wife who never left his side, and Abby skimmed it in the restaurant. There was no mention of how long they had been married (three months). As they talked about their trials, she and Ray used *we* constantly, meaning the two of them. They sounded plucky and happy, as if adversity had made them close.

Walt studied his wineglass for a while. "Why did he do it? Do you understand? Why did he cut you off like that?"

Abby had no answer at first. But she tried. "I think he felt he had permission, like a dying heart means never having to say you're sorry. And he needed something big, a great male fantasy, to get him through it. Of course he also needed someone to take care of him. I should have figured out a way to be the one."

Walt shook his head. "It wasn't because he needed a nurse. He told me he wanted to marry her a couple of years ago."

Abby hid behind her water glass, sorry he had felt the need to clear that up. She could see the shine begin in her own eyes, light refracted through salt water. So marriage meant nothing.

Eventually she said, "So he's happy now, with his young wife."

Walt looked surprised. "Happy? No. He's not happy. I bet he wakes up every day and thinks, 'Where am I?'"

SHE DIDN'T THINK that Walt was right—if Ray had gone on wanting to marry Tory, why did he ask her to move out and come back to Abby for a while?

But Abby blew it after that—she had been delusional, she could see that now. After she left Miami that last time, she had really believed he would come back, and it had sustained her, for almost a year. But it was a year in which he got too sick, and Abby wasn't there. She'd abandoned him, for what? For failing to introduce her one time as his wife, when she should have gone on leave and moved to Florida to care for him. She should have put up with Tory's proximity. Maybe then when Ray moved her to Harvard, she would have stayed.

Abby hated when people used *fight* and *struggle* and *battle* in reference to something personal, an overblown military metaphor. But she should have fought for him. She should have put away her hurt, armored herself, and waded in to fight to save his life. Instead she was the princess with the pea under her mattress, and because of that she was alone at sixty-three, childless, and close to washed-up socially.

But she had friends, a few—Ginger here, Nell in New York, Clarice and Walt in Providence. One thing for sure, she would never take anyone for granted again. She would appreciate every second that she spent with friends.

"MAYBE HE'LL GET a heart that works this time," her friends liked to quip, long after that ceased to be original.

Late January, three months after his heart collapsed, Tory's updates were about complications from the vacuum cleaner, which had put him in the hospital several times. "We have expanded the parameters for a heart. Because he is so thin, he could take a woman's heart now, and we've widened the age range."

Abby texted him anxiously. "This is going on too long. It's horrible to think of you hooked up to that machine every second of the day, making that tocking sound."

"Yes, it's obnoxious. But I'm alive and this ordeal could end anytime. Thank you for your concern. I hope you're well," he wrote back, just as he probably did to unknown well-wishers and donors every day.

February 15, Abby was in New York. Her publisher was hosting a benefit for Ray at St. Mark's, and this time she was invited to come read his work. Three hundred people showed up, lots of them his friends or hers, and all the friends hugged her.

Exhausted from weeping and hugging and grinning, she had just returned to her hotel room, about to meet people in the bar downstairs, when her phone rang.

It was Walt. "He got a heart."

Abby started to cry all over again, grinning wide. "When? How? Tell me!"

"Last night. Twenty-two-year-old guy from Tallahassee. They had Ray on the table with his chest open by the time they flew it down, and when they put it in him, it started beating on its own right away. Very good sign, apparently. It was an eight-hour surgery, and he'll be unconscious for a while. But it's about as good as it can get."

Abby raced downstairs, eyes streaming, wanting to tell the world.

She had a vision of Ray, on the day when they would let him stand up from his wheelchair, feeling better than he had in years. She could see his face, just the way it was in a picture his mother had showed her. He was six years old and sitting on a chair by a Christmas tree, in candy-striped feet pajamas, grinning with delight.

His face had looked that way again on a Christmas eve thirty years later, in Morgantown. A few months before, they had gone to Boston, and at the Museum of Fine Arts they saw a little elegant bronze snake from ancient Greece, which Ray had loved. Abby had secretly ordered a replica of it, hid it away, and wrapped it for Christmas.

She could never surprise him with a gift—he always figured them out. Curious as any kid, he'd snoop around wrapped packages until he knew. But the little narrow box under the tree stumped him, though he had poked and sniffed at it for days.

Finally, on Christmas eve, as she lay in the tub and he stood next to it to pee, his face had suddenly beamed out that six-year-old's delight.

"The little snake!" he cried. "You got me the little snake!"

RAY GOT BETTER, left the hospital, and he still wrote to Abby often in a friendly way. Every night she dreamed they were still married, and he was there. She understood her subconscious might always be married to him.

One night, after such a dream, she got out of bed, opened the French windows in the dining room, and stood there, breathing in the night. It had rained that day, and the air was clear and fresh. A bright moon slowly crested the black hill above her, luminous and so big she could see dark seas in it. Beauty hurt, and it seemed as if it always would.

In the morning, she looked around the place. His study was still packed with shelves of books and CDs, his filing cabinets, a closet full of clothes. She went to a packaging store and spent some of her scarce funds on twenty white boxes, giant rolls of tape, and brightly colored markers. *Ray's Poetry Books, A to C,* she wrote on the first one and started to pack them in. Box after box, she filled them up and labeled them.

She left the boxes in his study, with the furniture he wanted, moving everything else out of that room, so movers could make estimates. She got three, picked one, and scheduled it for early summer, when Ray might be well enough to receive it.

When she wrote and asked if June 1 would work for the delivery, he sounded alarmed. "Shouldn't you show me the estimates and let me decide?"

"I'm paying for it," she wrote back. It was the least she could do for him.

"Wow, Abby, that's very generous of you."

He never called her Beanie now, but it didn't matter anymore.

Had she been ambivalent to him? Maybe. For sure when he was shouting at her, bossing her around. Did he treat Tory that way? She would be sad for him, if so—anyone would be ambivalent to that. But probably his new quiet self would not. And if Tory adored him, if she worshipped him the way that Sateesh and Gloria did, they would be home free forever.

Before the end of that school year, Abby lost her platinum pen. One minute she was walking with it on the fourth floor of Wheeler Hall, down a long shining brown corridor, thinking, "I shouldn't have this in my hand," and the next it was gone. She reported it lost to the campus police, but though it had "A. McCormick-Stark" engraved on it, no one ever turned it in. Someone, somewhere, was now writing with her lovely thousand-dollar pen. The one Ray Stark had given her for twenty-five years of faithful service, before he retired her from his life.

Sometimes she opened a cookbook and found a note that he had left. He hated quiche and claimed that girls used to feed it to him. Abby didn't like it, either, but one day she noticed a recipe for it, annotated in Ray's print: As a final preparation step, he wrote, "Smother in pork chops, bake two hours." Another recipe called for canned tomatoes, and her own writing said, "Use fresh." The next ingredient was basil, and Ray had written, "Use hundred year old."

One brilliant, sunny day in June, she backed her car out of the garage and used the clicker to try to close the door, but it popped back up repeatedly. Finally she got out and used her hand to steady it as it went down. It closed.

As she walked back up the slope of driveway, something caught her eye, carved in the sidewalk—curious, she bent over to see what it was. It was a heart, crudely drawn with a stick, and in it were the letters

**RS**

**+**

**AMcC**

Abby got onto her knees and traced the lines with a fingertip. When did he do that, and why had she never noticed it? She could not recall when the sidewalk was redone, but it must have been long ago. They had been married seventeen years when they moved here, and Ray had left this small romantic gesture for her to find some day. It was amazing she had never seen it—she often worked in the garden next to it, planting and weeding. Her condo had come with one of the three parking spaces in the building's garage, and she went in and out of it by car and bike every day. She ran on this sidewalk. She must have been willfully oblivious.

Now the cement heart was the last of them that was permanent. She imagined Ray younger, handsome, mischievous, his chest unscarred, his heart intact, finding a stick and drawing it. She stayed on her knees for a long time, as dog walkers stepped around her, headed for the park. Then she got back in the car and drove away.